THE GREATEST FIREFIGHTER STORIES NEVER TOLD

THE GREATEST FIREFIGHTER STORIES NEVER TOLD

Mike Santangelo, Mara Bovsun,
and Allan Zullo

**Andrews McMeel
Publishing**

Kansas City

02 03 04 05 06 VAI 10 9 8 7 6 5 4 3 2 1

ISBN: 0-7407-2820-2

Library of Congress Control Number: 2002103761

*To the firefighters who lost
their lives in the terrorist attacks
on September 11, 2001,
and to all firefighters everywhere
who risk their lives every day.*

Contents

Acknowledgments

We wish to thank all the firefighters who graciously consented to be interviewed for this book.

We also greatly appreciate the help of Chief Jack Lerch and Lieutenant Dan May at the New York City Fire Department's Mand Library; firefighter Jerad Allis of the FDNY public affairs department; Frank Gribben, NYC deputy fire commissioner for public information; Vinnie Bollon, senior vice president of the International Association of Firefighters; Bill Kugelman, president of the Chicago Firefighters Union; Dominic Barbera, president of the Dade County Firefighters Union; Reverend John McNallis, historian of the Chicago Fire Department; retired Chicago firefighter Richard Scheidt; Chris Godek, former NYC deputy fire commissioner for public information; and Chief Paul Christian of the Boston Fire Department.

Introduction

FIRE POWER

After the terrorist attacks of September 11, 2001, one group of Americans stood out to the world as a symbol of courage and self-sacrifice: the members of the New York City Fire Department.

Three hundred forty-three FDNY Fire and Rescue personnel and six Emergency Medical Services technicians were among the 2,825 killed on that horrible day. Many of the doomed firefighters were off duty when they heard the news that two hijacked planes had crashed into the World Trade Center towers. These firefighters didn't wait for orders. Instead, they grabbed their turnout gear and dashed to the sounds of sirens, the smell of smoke, the sight of flames.

For many Americans, 9-11 was the first time they really thought about the bravery and courage of firefighters not only in New York but in their own hometowns. People no longer took for granted the intrepid men and women in fire departments across

Introduction

the country who risk their lives every day, and are on call 24/7 battling everything from a towering inferno to a smoldering trash bin.

Firefighters know that no blaze is predictable; no day on the job is ordinary. What they don't know for sure is what heartache or danger they will face when they rush out on a call. Will they discover a severely burned child curled up in the corner of a charred bedroom or will they be bombarded by flaming debris from a falling ceiling? Will they save a life or recover a body? Will they get hugs of thanks from grateful survivors or give hugs of condolences to victims' relatives?

After they don ninety pounds of gear and equipment, including flame-resistant turnout coats, heavy steel-soled boots and breathing packs, will they be running up the stairs of a burning skyscraper or running for their lives from a collapsing building?

To some people, it might seem foolhardy to charge into the flames to rescue someone you never saw before and may never see again. It's not that firefighters don't think about the danger. They're human and don't want to die, just like everyone else. But unlike most everyone else, they do what has to be done despite their fears.

That's why, as you'll see in this book, firefighter Joseph Clerici ignored pleas from his partners and

Introduction

low-crawled through a blazing apartment, risking death, while desperately groping in the dense smoke for a child who was assumed dead . . . firefighter John Traphagen leaped into a smoke-filled elevator shaft of a burning high-rise and shinnied down a cable to a red-hot elevator in a valiant rescue attempt . . . firefighter Bill Shea jumped fifteen feet down into a pit of fire without a plan of escape because to do nothing meant certain death for a trapped victim.

"When you hear somebody calling to you for help, you become like Superman," says Doug Jewett, a Miami firefighter and specialist in disaster rescue.

Gripping acts of heroism can happen anywhere at any time—a hotel in Chicago, a harbor in New York, a runway near Miami, a high-rise in Dallas. There are thousands of great firefighting stories. The stories featured here are representative of the amazing accounts of firefighter valor that aren't well known, have been long forgotten, or only received local media coverage. They involve big blazes and small ones, yet they all have one thing in common: the awesome danger that firefighters face. In most cases, we based these stories on personal interviews with the firefighters and witnesses; for other stories, we relied on firsthand reports in fire department archives.

In this book, you'll read about astonishing rescues spurred by fast thinking and quick improvising

Introduction

by firefighters who would never have considered doing what they did if lives weren't at stake. For instance, Matt Moseley dangled from a helicopter rope over a raging inferno to pluck a man off a melting crane. Charles Kamin tossed terrified children out of a burning second-story classroom as it reached its flash point because there was no time to carry them down the ladder.

You'll see that saving lives often requires not only strength and skill but psychology too. It's especially true when encountering people who, during a fire, either become paralyzed with fear or lose all reason, turning a typical rescue—if there is such a thing—into a bizarre adventure. Among such accounts: the rescued woman who kept running back into her blazing apartment and the man who climbed the wrong way down a ladder.

Some of the stories in this book reveal why firefighters need nerves forged under pressure. For example, undercover fire marshal Tommy Russo remained coolheaded even as a knife was held to his throat by an arsonist. Rescuer Doug Jewett kept his wits while searching for survivors deep inside the unstable rubble of an earthquake-flattened building, knowing full well the next tremor could crush him.

You'll also read about firefighters who put their lives at risk simply by doing what's right, like New

Introduction

York fireman Jay Jonas and his men. Under orders to evacuate immediately, they were running down the stairs of the North Tower of the World Trade Center when they came upon an exhausted woman on the twentieth floor. They refused to abandon her even though they knew they might not get out of the building in time. They were still with her inside the North Tower when it collapsed.

The day-to-day work of firefighters may never make the six o'clock news or the front page, earn a medal or even a thank-you. But you can bet the firehouse those dedicated men and women will be back on the job tomorrow, ready to plunge through a wall of flames when necessary, simply because that's who they are and that's what they do.

MIRACLE
IN THE
STAIRWELL

Against a stream of frightened and injured office workers pouring down the stairs, New York City Fire Department Captain Jay Jonas and his team of firefighters were methodically marching up toward the very deadly danger that was sending everyone else fleeing for their lives.

The eight sweaty, determined firefighters, each carrying about ninety pounds of protective gear and equipment, were heading up eighty grueling flights of stairs to battle a blaze they knew they could not douse and to save people they knew they could not reach.

And yet they kept on climbing and climbing the 110-story North Tower of the World Trade Center until . . .

"The building is collapsing!"

Two hours earlier, Jonas, who had worked the

overnight shift as Battalion Chief for the First Division in Lower Manhattan, was quietly sipping coffee in the station that houses Ladder 6 and Engine 9. Suddenly, the normal morning humdrum outside on the clear bright Tuesday morning of September 11, 2001, was shattered by a loud, shrieking roar overhead followed by an ominous boom seconds later.

At first he thought a truck had bottomed out on a pothole on the off-ramp of the Manhattan Bridge next to the fire station. But then the "beep-beep-beep-beep" squawked out of the intercom. Engine 9 firefighter Ray Hayden, who was in a different part of the station, said in a stunned voice, "A plane just crashed into the World Trade Center."

"What kind of plane?" Jonas asked into the intercom. "Was it a big plane or a small plane?"

"A real big plane, a commercial jet," replied Hayden.

Jonas paused for a fraction of a second and then coolly said, "Okay, let's turn both companies out."

Jonas had no orders yet from headquarters but he knew Ladder 6 and Engine 9 were second-alarm units. *If a jet hit one of the towers, they're going to call for a second alarm and more,* he reasoned. *I can't wait.*

As the firefighters scrambled onto their two rigs, Jonas heard a "10-60" coming over the department radio—the signal for a major disaster. From his seat on the right hand side of the ladder truck, the six-foot-one, 260-pound firefighter barked to the driver, "Let's go and get there fast!"

Seconds later, Jonas saw the stricken South Tower belching thick black smoke, its upper floors ablaze. "Man, will you look at that," Jonas murmured in awe as the truck turned right and raced toward the Battery. "I can't believe this. Look at those big, gaping holes in the tower."

I wonder how bad this is going to be, he thought. Then he started calculating. *It seems that about twenty stories are on fire. Each one of the tower floors is a square acre so I'm looking at twenty acres of fire. I don't think we're going to put this out.*

Jonas knew that however it turned out, this was going to be the fire of his life.

The captain started thinking about what he was going to do when they arrived at the scene. *There's an awful lot of smoke and flames. No sense making any strategic decisions here. We'll just go up and start pulling people out.* That's when reality took hold and he realized this was not a fire that was going to be extinguished by his men's hoses.

As his fire truck raced downtown, the driver had to weave in and out of traffic, but it wasn't vehicular. Tens of thousands of office workers were fleeing uptown across Vecsey Street, away from the horror at the WTC. *I've never seen so many people moving*

in one direction, Jonas thought. The only time he had witnessed anything like this was during the New York Marathon.

With sirens wailing from all directions, Jonas's two companies parked just south of the north walk-way on West Street, a bridge that linked the towers with the World Financial Center. As he and his men jumped off their vehicles and started grabbing their tools, they were bombarded by falling debris, mostly bits of office furniture, glass, paper, and ash. Jonas ordered the men to take shelter under the bridge and then kept watch until he could see a letup in the rain of rubble.

"Ready, set, go!" Jonas shouted moments later. Then he and his men sprinted to the truck to get their gear and raced back under cover as the next salvo of flaming debris fell. After three runs, the fire-fighters were ready to enter the burning building.

As Jonas came through the front door, he encountered emergency medical technicians tending to two office workers who were suffering from third-degree burns. "Where were they?" Jonas asked the medics.

"They came off the elevators from the upper floors," one EMT answered.

Jonas cringed, knowing how difficult his job was going to be, trying to reach a fire more than eighty stories up. He reported to the emergency command post, which had been set up in the lobby. "The elevators are out," Chief Peter Hayden told him. "That means your men are going to have to walk up."

While he was standing in line with other fire commanders, Jonas saw a big black shadow moving outside and then heard a massive explosion.

"A second plane just hit the other tower!" shouted a firefighter as he rushed in the doorway.

Everybody in the lobby stopped talking and gazed at one another in shock and disbelief. "Oh my God, they're trying to kill us!" Jonas exclaimed. *How many more planes will attack us?*

Chief Hayden then told Jonas, "Just go upstairs and do the best you can."

Looking at his seven firefighters from Ladder 6 and Engine 9, Jonas told them as bluntly and honestly as he could, "We're going to be lucky if we get out of this alive."

The men stared at each other, took a couple of deep breaths and then wished each other good luck. "I hope you make it," Jonas said softly. Then he cleared his throat and hollered, "Okay, let's go to work!" With a slight wave of his arm, he led his men to the "B" stairway, the only one that went from the lobby all the way up to the fire floors.

The men—clad in heavy boots, turnout coats, helmets, and masks and carrying oxygen tanks, rope, axes, and other equipment—entered the crowded stairs and began a rigorous climb that would test their physical and mental limits. They knew they had to pace themselves during their difficult ascent to avoid being too exhausted to fight fire or save lives, including their own.

To a man, the thought that dominated their minds was, *Are we heading to our deaths?* But they were members of the Fire Department of New York, "New York's Bravest." There was no backing down. They would follow their leader to hell if that's what needed to be done. Jonas turned around, gazed at his men behind him and swelled with emotion. *I'm so proud of these guys.*

The steps of the jam-packed "B" stairway were wide enough for only one single file heading down and another single file going up. Office workers grimly but hurriedly thundered down the stairs while the firefighters trudged up. *I can't believe how calm everybody is,* Jonas thought. *But why should I be surprised? These are New Yorkers. These are tough people.* Every now and then somebody would try to jump out of line and muscle down past the ascending firefighters, but cold stares and quick rebukes stopped the offenders in their tracks and they rejoined the line.

Instead of fleeing, several valiant office workers risked their lives by staying behind to help firefighters. On several floors, the workers had pried open vending machines and were standing by, handing out bottles of spring water to the heavily loaded firefighters who were making their way toward the flames on the top twenty floors.

Throughout most of the arduous climb for Jonas and his men, the lights stayed on, but the lower stairs were filled with water from burst pipes and sprinklers. The higher the men climbed, the stronger the smell of jet fuel and smoke. And the building began creaking, cracking, and moaning.

As they climbed above the tenth floor, they started seeing more victims of the terrorist attack. People suffering from compound fractures, severe lacerations, and burns hobbled down the stairs with the help of coworkers. Men had taken off their suit jackets and covered up women whose clothes and skin had been burned off. *It's awful to see,* Jonas thought, *but this really is New York at its best. Everybody is doing the right thing and they're doing it without being told.*

After a couple of rest stops, the firefighters made it to the twenty-seventh floor. Jonas knew it was vitally important for him to keep the men together under his direct command when working in a high-rise blaze. *I've got to make sure we operate as a unit and nobody gets lost,* he told himself. He realized he was missing two men who had lagged behind, so he went back and found them still climbing the stairs.

"We'll do this ten floors at a time from now on," he told his crew. "Ten floors and rest, then ten floors and rest until we get to the fire. No sense getting to the eightieth floor totally exhausted. Everybody take some water." His men still had bottles of the spring water that the workers had "borrowed" from the vending machines. As the men drank, they heard an increasingly loud rumble and felt a sudden tremble. It seemed like an earthquake.

"Dear God, don't tell me a third jet has struck the towers," Jonas muttered.

He could feel the building sway and quiver as the rumble turned into a roaring thunder. Then the lights went out for about twenty seconds. Another fire department officer, Captain Billy Burke of Engine 21, dashed to a nearby window and Jonas followed.

"All I can see is a white cloud," Jonas said, not quite knowing what he was staring at.

"Unbelievable. The other building just collapsed," Burke said in a flat monotone that masked the enormity of his words. The South Tower was now nothing but smoking rubble.

What now? Jonas thought, trying to digest the information. *If that building can collapse, so can this one.* The South Tower fell just fifty-four minutes after it was struck by a hijacked jetliner. It was 10 A.M., and the North Tower was still standing seventy-five minutes after it was attacked. *How long will it be before this one comes down too?*

Jonas could no longer ignore the growing number of widening cracks zigzagging on the walls and the incessant groaning of the steel girders. He could no longer justify risking the lives of his men when the threat of the building caving in seemed imminent. His heart wanted to go on, but his gut told him otherwise. "Okay, we're getting out of here," he told his men. "Let's start down."

Jonas felt a little uneasy about his decision because the command center hadn't issued any retreat order. But he also knew that because he was on the edge of radio range, which was between twenty-five to thirty stories, it was quite possible he might not have heard such an order if it had been given.

When the men turned around and headed down, Jonas now brought up the rear. They waited for him on the twentieth floor where firefighter Bill Butler was talking to a fatigued, heavyset woman. "What's she doing here?" Jonas asked him.

Her name was Josephine Harris and she was a week shy of her sixtieth birthday. With great effort, she had made it down from her office on the seventy-third floor with assistance from some co-workers. But when the South Tower fell, they had made the difficult decision to leave her and had fled down the stairs. Josephine, who had problems walking on good days on level ground, was physically spent after hiking down fifty-three floors to escape the fire. Breathing heavily and leaning on the railing, the exhausted woman couldn't move anymore on her own.

Oh, lord, she's just standing there, Jonas thought. *We can't leave her here alone.* His visions of a quick escape from the burning, weakening building faded from his mind.

One of the men asked Jonas, "Hey, Cap, what do you want us to do with her?"

"We take her with us," Jonas replied.

His response was met with a unanimous nod from all seven of his men. Butler put Josephine's arm over his shoulder while four other firefighters grabbed his gear. A sixth firefighter walked ahead of Butler to make sure the way was cleared for the company's newest member.

We're going at a snail's pace, thought Jonas as the group inched its way toward the lobby and safety. He knew they needed to move faster, but they couldn't. A mental clock was ticking in the back of his head, warning him that time was running out.

Twice, Jonas's men stood aside to allow other firefighters to scurry past them down the stairs. But his group remained together as a unit to help Josephine. By now nobody was heading up and everybody was trying to escape from what they expected to be a second disastrous collapse.

"Hey, Faust, it's time to go!" Jonas shouted to firefighter Faustino Apostol, a chief's aide and driver, who was standing on the seventeenth floor landing.

"Not now, Cap. I've got to wait for the chief," Faust answered with a smile.

On the fifteenth-floor landing, Jonas paused briefly to talk to Mike Warchola, a firefighter from Ladder 5 who was treating a man who had collapsed with chest pains. "Let's go!" Jonas ordered. "This building is about to fall."

"We'll be all right, Cap, you've got your civilian and I've got mine," Warchola shot back.

Jonas's little company kept creeping its way down. Somewhere below the tenth floor they were joined by Battalion Chief Rich Picciotto who bellowed through his bullhorn, "Everybody out! Get out!"

Picciotto told Jonas that within minutes after the collapse of the South Tower, the "get out as fast as you can" order had been issued. Jonas's hunch was right.

But Jonas couldn't move any faster without abandoning Josephine. *If I leave Josephine here, I'll spend the rest of my life in an institution from guilt. I just can't do it.* His men were thinking the same thing because all of them stayed with the woman who was now sobbing in pain. Each step was excruciating for her until finally at the fourth floor landing Josephine slumped to the ground.

Jonas went over and told her gently, "You've got to keep going, Josephine. We're almost out of here."

But all the bushed woman could do was shake her head, sending little droplets of tears in all directions down her cheeks.

"If I can get a good chair we can put you in it and carry you down fast," Jonas told her. Then he and his men pried open a locked office door and he darted into a huge deserted room. He ran from one end of the office to the other, desperately searching for a solid chair. But all he could find were swivel chairs, and they wouldn't work to transport Josephine to safety. *We'll just have to carry her. There's no other way.*

As he hurried back to the door, Jonas felt an odd sensation that quickly turned into terror. The floor he was standing on was jiggling in ripples as if it had suddenly turned to Jell-O. "Here we go!" he yelled. "It's coming down!"

He lunged for the door that led to the landing where his firefighters were waiting for him. But the door wouldn't open. The shifting of the building and the rippling of the floor had jammed it shut. *I'm a goner,* Jonas thought.

Just then a massive gust of wind whooshed down the stairway. The force from the collapse of the building was shoving air down the stairwell at hurricane-like speeds.

Suddenly the jammed door burst open and, in stunned amazement, Jonas watched a terrifying scene play out in front of him: The rush of air picked up one of his firefighters, 190-pound Matt Komorowski and his ninety pounds of gear, and flung him like a rag doll two floors down the steps. (Incredibly, he suffered no broken bones, although he had badly bruised every rib.) Battalion Chief Picciotto was also hurled downstairs by the wind.

Meanwhile, Josephine lay on the floor with Butler and fireman Tom Falco holding her as the stairway wobbled and swayed. The rest of the firefighters in the group crouched low and gripped the stair railing as the air rushed past them.

Before anyone had time to think, the stairway reverberated with a frightening series of unbelievably loud rapid booms. BANG . . . BANG . . . BANG . . . BANG . . . BANG.

Jonas's heart sank. He knew exactly what those horrible bangs meant: the floors of the 110-story building were pancaking. As he had feared, the building was collapsing.

Damn, we didn't make it, he thought. *We came so close to getting out. It just wasn't enough.* As he listened to the floors slam onto one another, he wondered, *When is the big beam or slab of concrete coming to crush me?* Feeling doomed, he shook his head in resignation and then pictured his wife, Judy, in his mind. He wanted Judy to be his last thought on earth.

After thirteen horrifying seconds, the deafening bangs stopped and everything went silent. Jonas, who had been scrunched into a ball to protect himself from the falling debris, relaxed his body. *My God, I survived! I guess the end is not coming just yet.*

Jonas could hear coughing and gagging in the stairway, which was caked with dust and debris. With his fingers, he scraped thick dust from his face and eyes so he could look around and then he took a roll call of his crew. Everybody, including Josephine, answered "Here," causing Jonas to breathe a sigh of relief.

It's a miracle! We're all alive after all that, he thought. *But what's going to happen to us next?*

Also standing on the shaky fourth-floor landing with Jonas's group were a lieutenant from Engine 16, another firefighter, and a Port Authority cop. Chief Picciotto remained on the second-floor landing, where he and Komorowski had ended up after being blown down. The stairs from the second floor to the third floor were gone.

Although virtually the entire building had collapsed, Jonas didn't believe at the time that it was a total destruction because it happened so fast.

Miracle in the Stairwell

Incredibly, the only section that hadn't pancaked completely was the "B" stairway.

Suddenly over his radio, Jonas heard a "Mayday" from Mike Warchola, the firefighter who had stayed on the fifteenth-floor landing to help the man with the chest pains. In a shaky voice, Warchola told Jonas that he was trapped in the rubble.

Although the stairs above him were unstable and strewn with debris, Jonas worked his way toward the fifteenth floor, hoping to free Warchola. But when Jonas reached the twelfth floor, he was stopped by tons of rubble. The stairway no longer existed above that point. There was only a jumble of twisted metal and chunks of concrete. He frantically tried to search for an opening, but it was hopeless.

He's my friend and there's not a thing I can do to help him, Jonas thought. *It's bad enough when it's somebody you never met, but this is a guy who went to my wedding.*

Reluctantly, Jonas headed back down the stairs to be with his men. The dust was so thick from the collapse that he could see only about four feet in front of him. *I hope there are no big holes in this stairway,* he thought.

When he arrived at the fourth-floor landing, he heard Chief Picciotto shouting up to him from the second floor. "This stairway is a little shaky, you don't want to go charging up and down." Then he cautioned that the third-floor landing and first-floor landing were gone. The only way to get down to the second-floor landing was to shinny along the railing.

Jonas told his men to cut their lights and radios to save power. He and Picciotto then used their radios to try to contact rescuers below.

"I'll get on the command frequency," Picciotto said.

"And I'll tune into the tactical channel," said Jonas.

After about forty minutes of trying to make contact without a response, Jonas was wondering if anyone would find them. *This is a sixteen-acre site,* Jonas thought. *It's not going to be easy to zero in on one place now that all the landmarks are gone.* Then over the radio he heard the voice of Deputy Chief Tom Haring say, "We have your location. And we have an army working on getting you out."

Jonas tried to keep his voice calm and professional while giving the men outside as much information as he could about where he and his people were trapped.

Then Battalion Chief Bill Blaich got on the radio and told him, "It's a real mess out here, so it's going to take some time to get to you. But I've got the entire off-duty platoon of Ladder 11 and Ladder 6 looking for you. We'll get you out."

These guys are the best, thought Jonas. *I've got*

the best looking for us and we're going to be all right. He filled in his men on the status of their rescue. "We may be here for a while, so let's explore and see if we can find something that will help us."

The firemen broke open doors and found a non-working toilet and a sprinkler system pipe that looked like it might have some water in it. *Well, that's something,* thought Jonas as he retreated back onto the stairway. All that was left of one floor they had entered was a six- by four-foot void in the debris.

When Jonas looked over to Josephine he could see she was hunkered down and not crying anymore. *If it hadn't been for her, we would be dead right now,* he thought. He realized that Josephine had slowed them down just enough so that they were between the second and fifth floor when the building came down. Had they left her and run for their lives, they all would have been killed. *By saving her we unknowingly were saving ourselves.*

Josephine had been quiet and when Jonas walked close to her, she looked up and tried to smile. But then her lips trembled. "I'm scared," she confessed and began to cry.

"Darling, we're all a little scared right now," he told her. "But we're going to get out of this place soon."

Jonas looked at his watch and realized that more than three hours had passed since the tower collapsed. It hadn't seemed nearly that long.

Over the radio, he learned that massive blazes in No. 6 World Trade Center and No. 7 were getting worse. Men were shouting that the fires were getting away from them and they needed more help. Every now and then somebody would warn of a possible new collapse of one of the buildings. Several times explosions were audible on the radio but he didn't need to have his hand-held to hear the blasts.

While his group waited for help, Jonas turned to the Port Authority cop who had joined up with his company and asked, "Hey, do you have a cell phone?"

"I have two cell phones, but I can't raise anyone in town."

Although it was virtually impossible to get a call through to anyone in the city, the phones were able to make contact with the suburbs. Firefighter Billy Butler dialed his wife in Orange County, an upstate suburb of New York City. "We're alive, honey, but we're trapped," Butler said. "Call the firehouse and tell them where we are."

Then he asked her to call Jonas's wife with the news that Jonas was safe.

A few minutes later one of the men looked up and said, "Hey, I see a beam of light." The thick dust from the collapse had finally cleared enough to reveal a huge hole high in the stairwell leading to what should have been the inside of the building.

Miracle in the Stairwell

"Guys, there used to be about a hundred stories above that hole and now we can see sunlight," said the awestruck captain, trying to comprehend the scene of utter devastation.

Finally, firefighters from Ladder 43 arrived. They secured a rope and rigged a hitch so that the trapped group could climb down one by one. Jonas and firefighters Tom Falco and Sal Dagostino stayed with Josephine.

"We made it, Josephine," Jonas told the drained, tear-stained woman. "You can stop being scared now." He knew he and his exhausted men couldn't carry her down the rope. They would wait for a fresh crew from Ladder 43 who would lower her down on a stretcher.

A few minutes later Lieutenant Glen Rowan, the Ladder 43 boss, appeared on the landing. "You guys are relieved," he said.

Rowan briefed Jonas on what had happened and Jonas told him about the Maydays he had picked up on his radio. Finally Jonas followed his last two men down the rope to the top of a three-story pile of steaming debris that was once a shining building.

We're out! Jonas told himself. *Oh, God, this is unbelievable.*

Soon he wasn't thinking about anything other than keeping his balance as he made his way over the dust-coated beams that were as slippery as ice. But the beams weren't the only obstacles. Jonas started hearing the sound of gunfire. The CIA, FBI, and Secret Service had offices in the World Trade Center No. 6, which was now burning furiously, setting off the stockpile of ammo. *That's just great. All I need now is to be hit by some stray shot.*

The collapse had created a three-story-deep trench amid the debris, and Jonas and his men would have to descend into it and climb back out before they were safe. "Keep moving, keep moving," he urged his men. "You don't have to go fast but keep going." He could see some of them were about to fall from sheer exhaustion. "Your wife and kids are on the other side of that trench," Jonas said, patting firefighter Mike Meldrum on the shoulder. Meldrum had suffered a concussion when the building went down and was having trouble walking.

They were four hundred yards from safety, but every step was agony for the weary firefighters. When they were down inside the hollow, none of them thought they would have the strength to climb out the other side.

"Oh, look at that. Isn't that beautiful!" Jonas declared when he saw the heads of police and firefighters over the rim of the trench. Soon ropes were sent down to his men, who were then hoisted up the far side to waiting ambulances.

Miracle in the Stairwell

"We made it, Cap," exulted Falco as medics escorted him to an ambulance.

"You're next," another EMT said to Jonas.

"No. I've got to report to the chief first," he said and started walking toward the fire command center.

On top of an engine stood Chief Hayden shouting orders to dozens of fresh men arriving on the scene.

"Chief!" Jonas hollered above the din. At first Hayden didn't hear him, so Jonas shouted again, louder, three or four times.

Finally Hayden turned toward him and broke out in a wide grin when he recognized the grime-covered worn-out captain.

"We made it!" Jonas said.

"Jesus, it's good to see you," Hayden said.

"Yes, sir, it's good to be here," Jonas said, snapping his sharpest salute.

Jonas and his men had survived. But his good friends, firefighters Mike Warchola and Faustino Apostol, who he had seen in the stairwell, weren't so lucky. They were among the 343 New York firefighters who so heroically gave their lives.

As for Josephine, she was able to walk out of the hospital in a few days, grateful to the firefighters who had saved her life . . . and grateful that she had unwittingly saved their lives.

LEAP OF FAITH

Lieutenant John Traphagen faced a daunting challenge: He needed to rescue a woman trapped in an elevator on the twenty-eighth floor of a high-rise, a floor that was being consumed by fire. If he didn't do something quickly, she would be cooked to death.

That's when he conjured up an audacious rescue plan that put his own life in jeopardy.

The fire erupted near the top of the thirty-one-story Mercantile Bank Building in Dallas on November 18, 1961. Because it was a Saturday, most offices were empty, but there were some employees working that day, including elevator operator Joy Buckbee.

The elevators were cutting-edge technology at the time. A sensor system on each floor allowed a person to summon the elevator simply by placing his hand over a heat-sensitive circle without touching it. But because this sophisticated elevator system couldn't tell the difference between the heat from a person's hand and the heat from a fire, it carried her to mortal danger.

Buckbee had been in an elevator on a low floor when the fire broke out on the twenty-eighth floor. The heat of the flames summoned all the elevators to the burning floor, including the one she was in. When the elevator door opened, she faced a wall of flames. She couldn't get the elevator to go up or down because by now all the elevators had ceased to function. Buckbee was trapped in what was now an oven with an uncontrollable, rising thermostat. And there was nothing she could do.

When Traphagen arrived on the scene, he was briefed on the deadly situation. Time was of the essence. But he and his firemen couldn't use the elevators. They would have to climb the stairs.

Oh, Lord, this is going to be some uphill charge, he thought. Then he ordered his men, "Follow me." On the stairway Traphagen and his group joined a procession of firefighters, some carrying hoses and others armed with axes, steel bars, or pikes, who were working their way up toward the fire floor. "It's a long way up, so pace yourselves," Traphagen told them. "You want to have something left to fight the fire."

Leap of Faith

To himself he muttered, "Keep it moving. That woman in the elevator hasn't got very long. If we can't get her out of the box she's in, she'll die."

His main worry was exhaustion and lack of breathable air for himself and the other firefighters. They all had Scott Packs with them—cylinders of compressed air that would give their lungs a boost. But with the exertion of climbing the stairs, most of the men would quickly use up the twenty to thirty minutes of air in their packs.

As he climbed the stairs, Traphagen tried to drag from his memory everything he knew about the bank headquarters. He had spent hours studying firefighting manuals and blueprints of the city's major buildings before taking the test for lieutenant the year before. He had even read manuals while sitting on the beach during his summer vacation. From the time he had joined up in 1953, being a member of the Dallas Fire Department was much more than just a job to him. It was his life.

Meanwhile, Buckbee was suffering in a metal oven heated by a fire that had fully engulfed the twenty-eighth floor. The only reason she was still alive was that the elevator shaft was acting like a chimney. Fresh air was being sucked up from the bottom of the building by an updraft with hurricane-force winds. The upward rush of air not only was giving the trapped woman just enough oxygen to survive but it was keeping the elevator car from bursting into flames.

After Traphagen and his panting firefighters reached the twenty-eighth floor, stubborn flames filled the hallway. More than a dozen firefighters had already hooked up hoses to the building's standpipe system and were shooting high-pressure jets of water on the flames. But the blaze wasn't giving up easily, and from the look of the smoke and the feel of the heat Traphagen knew Buckbee's time was running perilously short.

"We'll never get to that elevator in time from here," Traphagen said to his men. He figured it would take ten minutes before the firefighters fought their way down the hall to the elevator. If the fire surged up, it could take longer. If he was going to save Buckbee, he was going to have to figure out another way.

What's going through her mind? he wondered. *She must be terrified in there, all alone and not knowing if anybody knows she's there or if anybody is coming to save her.*

Traphagen analyzed every possible escape route, searching his memory for everything he'd ever read in firefighting books, everything he'd ever learned. Nothing had prepared him for this.

There was only one option that he figured could possibly work: He would come in from above the flames through the elevator shaft, get down to the elevator roof, pry open the escape hatch on top, and lift Buckbee out. Then, both would be pulled out to an upper floor elevator door and to safety by his men.

As the officer in command, he had to swiftly work out the details of the plan and then execute it. His first problem was figuring out how to get down the shaft. Ladders weren't long enough, and his gear didn't include a rope. *I don't have much time. Once we get above the fire, I'll think of something to get me to the elevator.*

Traphagen gulped some fresh air from his Scott Pack and started to climb the stairs to the next floor. The air was thick with smoke because the fire had now spread to the twenty-ninth floor. "Let's try the next floor," he yelled to his men as he scrambled up to the next landing. On the thirtieth floor, just below the top floor, the air seemed clear enough to take a chance. "Okay, this is better. Let's get to the elevator shaft."

Using pry bars and axes, the firefighters forced open the metal doors to the elevator shaft. A blast of hot, smoky air slapped him in the face. "Oh, Lord, look at that," Traphagen muttered. A shrieking, violent updraft in the shaft was driving pitch black smoke from the twenty-eighth floor to the top of the shaft. The air was hot enough to roast wieners.

How can that woman still be alive? he thought. *If she's still breathing, she must be very close to being finished.*

The lieutenant hesitated, but for only a split second. "Go back down to the twenty-ninth," he ordered his men. "And get the door to the elevator shaft open as quickly as you can."

In answer to the puzzled look on their faces, Traphagen explained, "I'm going down the cable and I'll need you to pull me out."

He told them that once he got Buckbee out onto the roof of the elevator car, he would pass her up to them through the pried-open elevator door on the twenty-ninth floor. This plan hinged on the firefighters from the other companies extinguishing the flames on that floor so that his men could reach the elevator door. Otherwise he'd have to find a way to get up to the thirtieth floor with Buckbee in tow. No one—including Traphagen—thought he could ever climb back up the cable while holding onto the woman.

"Let's go!" Traphagen yelled. While his men hustled off to the floor below, he took a flying leap into the shaft and latched onto the metal elevator cable. He was immediately assaulted by a shrill roar, the stove-hot updraft, and biting smoke. It felt like he was in a tunnel that led straight to hell. Traphagen buried his face in the collar of his turnout coat to

Leap of Faith

shelter his skin from the intolerable heat and smoke. *This is no time to have second thoughts or doubts*, he told himself.

He eased his way down the cable, which was growing hotter by the second. Adding to his woes, the cable was so ragged it was ripping his gloves, heavy turnout coat, trousers, and boots with every move. *Guess I'm going to have to get a new outfit when this is through*, he thought.

Rather than dwell on the difficulties he faced, Traphagen tried to think positively. *This isn't so bad,* he told himself. *It's not too different from sliding down the pole in the firehouse.* He looked down but he couldn't see much through the smoke. *Thank God the fire hasn't broken through in the shaft. I don't see any signs of flames yet.* If fire did break through the shaft wall, Traphagen knew that he and Buckbee would burn to death.

All the way down Traphagen talked to himself to keep his mind off what he might find inside the elevator car. It also prevented him from thinking what would happen to him if his men couldn't open the elevator door on the twenty-ninth floor in time. *I know they'll do it,* Traphagen thought. *They're good men. But if they don't, they're going to have to break in a new lieutenant.* By now, the sharp metal strands of the cable had sliced deep into his hands, legs, and feet. Despite the pain from his lacerations, he continued his gritty descent, which was becoming increasingly difficult because his blood was trickling down the cable, making it slippery for him to grab.

The thickening, choking smoke hid the elevator car. *How much further?* he wondered. Just then his boot touched the top of the car. *At last!* Some of the stress that had tensed his body began to ease slightly.

"Now let's get her out, let's get her out, let's get her out," he repeated out loud to himself. He wondered what he would find inside. *Will she be conscious? Will she be hysterical? Will she have the presence of mind to be able to help me save her life?*

Another blast of hot, smoky air hit him in the face as he fumbled for the escape hatch, his bloody hands cramping from his struggle down the rope. *Have I got the strength to jump down into that car and then lift that woman back up here?* he wondered.

In the back of his mind, he was nagged with a gruesome thought that Buckbee might not even be alive. *Right now she could be just a corpse huddled in a corner of the elevator.*

Using a small metal pry bar, he wrenched the hatch off. His heart sank as he peered inside. *Like a bundle of rags,* he thought. Buckbee was curled in the corner on the floor of the smoke-filled chamber. She looked dead.

But he couldn't leave. He had to find out for

sure if she had died. Just as he was getting ready to jump down into the elevator, Buckbee twitched and slowly turned her head. Two big eyes, filled with terror, gazed up at him.

Now that's a frightened face, he thought. The woman was covered in soot from the smoke and she was near collapse from the lack of oxygen.

"Put your hands up and reach for me!" Traphagen shouted above the wail of the fire-driven wind rushing up the elevator shaft. "Reach up to me and I'll grab you and get you out of here!"

Buckbee didn't respond. She just stared at him.

"Don't worry, I do this sort of thing every day," he lied, trying to reassure her and thwart the panic he could see spreading across her face. She kept looking at him, as if she couldn't comprehend who he was or why he was there.

She's scared stiff and can't even move, he told himself. *Jeez, I'm going to have to go down there and get her. It's worse than an oven inside. How has she managed to survive this long?*

Traphagen was ready to jump into the chamber when Buckbee suddenly snapped out of her fear-induced paralysis. Without a word, she gradually stood up and raised her hands above her head, reaching for him. The look of terror was still etched on her face.

Oh thank you, lady! he thought as he leaned

over and clamped his gloveless, bloody hands around her wrists. "One yank and I can get you out of there," he told her as he began to haul her out of the baking elevator.

When he maneuvered her head and shoulders through the hatch, he heard the screech and thunk of metal being pried apart above him. He looked up and through the smoke, he saw two of his firefighters grinning at him from the open elevator door.

"Are you going to stay in there all day, Lieutenant?" one of his men yelled down.

Maybe some other time Traphagen would have laughed, but not this time. He could see that Buckbee was losing consciousness and needed oxygen immediately. "Cut the jokes and let's go!" he snapped to his men. He lifted Buckbee high enough for the firefighters from the floor above to snatch her to safety. Then the men helped him out of the shaft.

Wiped out from the ordeal and coughing from the heavy smoke he inhaled in the elevator shaft, Traphagen sucked in oxygen and rolled over in his mind what had just happened. His coat was shredded beyond repair, as were his boots. His gloves were so torn they had fallen off his hands down the shaft.

A few feet from where Buckbee was receiving oxygen, the medic turned to Traphagen and said, "She's going to be fine. She was right on the edge of being dead, but she's recovering nicely."

Traphagen couldn't help but think that had he been a minute slower running up the stairs, or if he had hesitated before taking a blind leap toward a smoke-shrouded cable, Buckbee would be in the morgue wagon right now.

It was a spectacular rescue in an otherwise ordinary fire. Buckbee recovered quickly in the hospital from smoke inhalation and the effects of heat. The damaged floors of the bank building were remodeled and the heat-sensitive elevator system was dismantled and replaced by a conventional system.

In August 1962, the hero firefighter became the first man to receive his department's Medal of Valor. It was pinned on him in a full-dress ceremony by a very grateful Joy Buckbee.

DEATH OF THE ANGELS

he student burst into Sister Mary Helaine's eighth-grade class at Our Lady of Angels Catholic School and shouted, "Sister, Sister! There's smoke in the hall!"

The nun peeked into the frighteningly hot, smoke-choked hallway and then slammed the door shut and closed the overhead transom. There was no way out. She and her students were trapped. As smoke began sneaking in through the cracks, she ordered, "Quick, get me some books to put around the door!"

The students did what they were told and then scrambled toward the windows and threw them open. Panicked classmates pressed against each other as they tried to gulp fresh air.

Down below, people from the neighborhood, alerted by the smoke, were futilely trying to break down a locked iron fence that blocked access to the school.

Several blocks away, Lieutenant Charles Kamin and four of his men from Hook and Ladder Company 35—one of the first stations to respond to the alarm—were barreling toward the address that had been called in to the fire dispatcher. But it was the wrong address.

Meanwhile, in Room 211, Sister Mary Helaine told her terrified students, "Children, let us pray."

It was the afternoon of December 1, 1958, a date that would forever be remembered as the day of the most heartbreaking fire in Chicago history.

Our Lady of Angels, a U-shaped two-and-a-half-story building of brick and timber joist construction built in 1910, was the center of activity in the modest, west-side neighborhood of predominantly Italian and Irish families. The school's overcrowded classrooms bulged with more than 1,600 children from kindergarten to eighth grade who were taught by twenty Sisters of Charity of the Blessed Virgin Mary Order and nine lay teachers.

About 2 P.M. on that fateful day—during an era when smoke detectors and sprinkler systems weren't required on older buildings like this one—a fire began in a trash barrel at the bottom of the school's northeast stairwell. (Fire investigators later suspected an arsonist set the blaze but no one was ever arrested.) It smoldered until the heat eventually broke a basement window, causing a rush of fresh air to turn the minor trash fire into a blowtorch that raced up the wooden stairs like a kid late for class. The blaze grew unchecked as it roared past the first floor, which had fire doors, to the vulnerable second floor, which did not.

Meanwhile, hot gases swirled up into the space between the roof and the ceiling of the second-floor classrooms of the north wing where six nuns and two lay instructors were teaching 329 children. There, superheated air sparked flames that eventually fell into the second-floor corridor from ventilator grilles in the north wing. The flames combined with dense smoke and gases, making the hallway impassable. Inside the classrooms, light fixtures and transom windows exploded before flames broke through the ceiling.

When the fire was finally detected, someone pulled the alarm. But the alarm alerted only those inside the building; it wasn't connected to the fire department. More than eight vital minutes passed before someone finally called in the fire—and gave the West Iowa Street address of the church rectory, located behind the school, rather than the North Avers Avenue address of the school.

The classrooms in the south wing and the first floor of the north wing were evacuated. But hundreds of students were trapped on the second floor of the north wing because they couldn't reach the school's only fire escape at the rear of the building.

When Hook and Ladder Company 35 arrived at the rectory, Lieutenant Kamin saw children screaming from the windows of the south wing of the school. "That's odd," he told a fellow fireman. "No smoke. There has to be a fire somewhere, otherwise why such panic?"

The firemen got the ladder out and were ready to rescue the frightened kids when Kamin heard shouts coming from the corner of the building: "The fire is on the other side! Go to the other side!"

Only then did Kamin realize that the children who were gathered by the windows of the south wing weren't in immediate danger; that the blaze was in the north wing. The confusion wasted only a couple of minutes, but if the thirty-eight-year-old fireman had learned anything during his eleven years on the job, it was that every second was precious. Minutes could be the difference between a little fire and a killer blaze, between life and death.

Quickly, Kamin and his men sprinted around the corner of the building where they saw frantic children hanging out of smoke-belching windows. To make matters worse, the firemen's path to the trapped students was blocked by an eight-foot-tall iron fence that stretched across a courtyard between the two wings. The fence had been locked to keep trespassers out during school hours.

No one was there to unlock it, so Kamin and his men, with the help of neighbors, burst through the gate by using a ladder as a battering ram. Then two of Kamin's men brought a safety net and ran under a window where petrified children were already jumping twenty-five feet to the frozen ground and writhing in pain from broken bones.

Seeing the net, students leaped out in droves, four and five at a time. The firemen would dump the kids out of the net and pull it tight for the next jumpers. Neighbors would help clear the kids from the net and escort them away from the building. Victims whose hair or clothes were smoldering were doused with water from garden hoses.

As the smoke thickened, the firemen couldn't move swiftly enough. The children were jumping out at an increasingly faster rate. Within minutes the net sagged under the weight of a pile of children hitting so quickly that it was impossible to clear off one child before another hit.

At other windows where there wasn't a safety net below, desperate children jumped anyway. Heroic firefighters and neighbors tried to catch the plummeting kids and even selflessly used their bodies to break the falls. For some firefighters and neighbors, their brave efforts meant a trip to the hospital with a broken bone, but with the satisfaction of knowing that they had saved lives.

Adding more confusion and despair, anxious parents rushed the police lines, hysterically trying to reach their children who were trapped in the building. Although many tried to help, others hampered the efforts of the firefighters.

Kamin looked up at another part of the south wing and saw students crammed at a second-story window, screaming and crying. They were the trapped eighth-graders from Sister Mary Helaine's class in Room 211.

Kamin slammed the twenty-six-foot ladder against the wall by the window, scurried up the rungs and looked in on a horrifying sight. About twenty students were jammed against the window, pushing so hard that the ones in front were being crushed against the windowsill, which was about four feet above the floor. They were wedged in tight, boys in front, most of the girls in back. Out of the corner of his eye, Kamin saw smoke snaking into the room from a door about ten feet away. The smoke was getting thicker and hotter by the second.

Then Kamin noticed something that made his blood run cold. The students' white shirts were changing color, going from white to tan, then growing darker like marshmallows over a campfire. The blistering heat was starting to burn their clothing.

Death of the Angels

Seconds, I have just seconds, Kamin thought. The burning clothes told him that in no time the room was going to reach a flash point in which everything—furniture, books, papers and children—would go up in one great white flame.

It'll take about fifteen seconds to get one kid down the ladder, and another ten to get back, Kamin thought. *I don't have that kind of time.*

In desperation, he did something that would have seemed unthinkable just minutes earlier. He reached into the room full of weeping students, grabbed a boy by the belt, lifted him up and yanked him out the window, letting him fall. In Kamin's mind, the boy at least had a chance of surviving a twenty-five-foot plunge; he had no chance of surviving in the classroom. Again, Kamin reached in, grasped a boy by the belt and pulled him out the window. *If I can move fast enough, maybe at least one will live, just one,* Kamin thought.

Inside the heat was becoming unbearable. *Any second, this room could go up,* Kamin told himself, trying to block out the sound of the children's screams. Still, he kept seizing children, dragging them out and dropping them, not even looking where they landed. He hoped that some would grab the ladder on the way down or would be caught by firefighters or neighbors who could break their fall. Kamin couldn't stop to think about it. *I just have to get them out.*

The eighth-graders were no lightweights, all weighing over one hundred pounds. Normally lifting that kind of weight with one arm would be beyond Kamin's strength, even though he was a well-conditioned firefighter. But a power he had never felt before surged through his muscles. He kept grasping kids, lifting them out the window, then tossing them down.

A frenzied girl who scrambled over the shoulders of her classmates climbed into Kamin's arms. He slung her behind him on the ladder.

Inside, the heat was getting so intense that a boy's glasses started to melt. And then, following a loud poof, Room 211 turned into a sea of flames and a cacophony of shrieks. The classroom had reached its flash point.

The flames seared Kamin's arms and forced him to close his eyes. With one last frantic grab, Kamin blindly reached in and pulled out one more child, a boy whose his shirt was in flames. Throwing the badly burned child over his shoulder, Kamin, who was in agony himself, retreated down the ladder to the pavement. Knowing there was nothing else he could, Kamin felt sick to his stomach. Twenty-six children were still inside, but there were no more screams coming from Room 211.

While Kamin was flinging children out the window, other companies rushed to the school. More than forty fire trucks jammed the streets, blocking the way for late arrivals, including Richard Scheidt and his men from Rescue 3. They abandoned their truck two blocks away and ran the rest of the way, each carrying an axe and pike-pull, a six-foot spear with a hook on one end that firemen use for wrenching down ceilings and walls in burning buildings.

When the men from Rescue 3 arrived at the scene, Scheidt gazed at the fire through the smashed iron gate in the courtyard and thought, *It looks like the gate to hell.* Two dozen firefighters were squeezing into the front doorway, trying to get into the burning building. *This could be my kids' school.* For a brief moment, Scheidt's thoughts turned to his three young children, each of whom was at that moment sitting in a classroom across town being taught by a nun, just like the students were at Our Lady of Angels until a few minutes ago. *Put your kids out of your mind. You've got a job to do.*

Scheidt took a deep breath, then joined the other firefighters who were swarming into the main entrance. Some were dragging hoses; others, like Scheidt, were wielding axes or pikes. All wore expressions of trepidation and consternation.

"Please let us get there in time, let them be alive," Scheidt murmured, the images of his own children embedded in his mind, no matter how hard he tried to push them out. He and the rest of Rescue

3 followed the hoses and the high-pressure streams of water in a step-by-step battle up the charred stairs against a wall of fire.

When they reached the second floor landing, twenty firefighters were manhandling hoses and trying to beat back the flames. But the stubborn fire would not give an inch without a fight.

Just several feet away, on the other side of the doors to the classrooms were trapped children and nuns. Scheidt knew they might die before the flames were pushed back beyond the doorways. Because firemen couldn't get through the fire to the kids until the flames were knocked down, there was only one other way to reach them.

"Chop through the wall!" boomed rescue squad commander Captain Harry Weeden.

Scheidt and his men started swinging their axes, sending up chunks of plaster and pieces of two-by-fours. He kept chopping away with such frenzy that he had no idea of what was happening around him. His whole focus and energy were directed to this one wall that separated him from the trapped children. He ignored the flames that were spreading across the ceiling, sending burning debris crashing down around the firemen.

Finally, they made a hole large enough for Scheidt to squeeze through. He hoped to find a group of children and a nun huddled in the corner alive. But even though he was a veteran firefighter, what he saw filled him with unspeakable horror. In a corner of the scorched room was a pile of dead children, their little limbs tangled around each other's burned bodies.

Before he could fully comprehend the horrible sight, he heard Captain Weeden shout, "Start chopping the wall to the next room! More kids are in there. Maybe some of them are alive."

Scheidt and his fellow firemen attacked the wall with their axes and pikes. "We gotta get to those kids, we gotta get 'em out," he said, furiously swinging his axe into the plaster. Within a few minutes, he burst through the wall, only to face another gut-wrenching sight. Nearly forty children, the entire class, were bunched together in a heap in the corner, lifeless. But none looked as though they had been burned.

Some of them might still be saved if I can just get them oxygen fast, Scheidt thought. He dropped his axe and ran to the mound of humanity. *If I move fast, maybe I can save at least one kid.*

None of the children were breathing, but they had escaped most of the flames. *It's possible that doctors could bring them back and get them breathing again.* Scheidt had seen it happen before. He peeled a boy off the pile and passed the unconscious child to another fireman. Then a girl, another girl, a boy. One by one, he hurriedly handed the children to firefighters, who scampered down the stairs to waiting ambulances.

At one point, Scheidt paused when he noticed a girl with unusually short hair. *How strange*, he thought as he looked at her sweet face. Then he realized she wasn't a child, but a young nun who had been teaching the class. He pictured what had probably happened: In their terror, the students tried to cling to her. As they collapsed from the heat, they pulled off her headdress, exposing the closely-cropped hair that showed she had forsaken vanity. Scheidt passed her body to a fireman and reached for another victim.

The firefighters raced through the smoke to bring the lifeless students from the second-floor classroom into the fresh air. Each hoped the unresponsive child he was carrying would miraculously be revived after a whiff of oxygen.

"This one still has pink cheeks!" Scheidt reported, as he scooped up a boy and darted down the stairs. "Maybe I'll get lucky, maybe I'll get lucky," he kept repeating as he pressed the limp body against his chest.

In the street, he handed the boy off to a doctor. But instead of trying to resuscitate the boy, the doctor took a quick look, shook his head and gave him to a policeman who was on the dead body detail. "Put him in the morgue wagon," the doctor ordered.

Death of the Angels

Dismayed but undeterred, the fireman thought, *Maybe the next one.* Every time Scheidt ran out of the burning building with a child in his arms, he kept hoping that maybe, just maybe, this one could be revived. Every time he turned over a lifeless child, he asked the doctor, "Aren't you going to try giving oxygen?" The answer was always the same: a shake of the head. It was too late.

For Scheidt the whole world seemed strangely silent and numb. He was in such a mental zone that he no longer heard the sirens wailing, the parents sobbing, the firemen shouting. He no longer felt the scorching heat, his straining muscles or his aching heart.

After at least a dozen trips up and down the stairs, there were no more bodies to carry out. Scheidt and the men of Rescue 3 had pulled out of the flaming classrooms nothing but fatalities. Not one survivor. The men had risked their lives for what turned out for them to be a recovery operation instead of a rescue mission.

Of the 329 children, six nuns, and two lay teachers trapped that horrible day in the second floor of the north wing, ninety-five died—fifty-five girls, thirty-seven boys, and three nuns. Dozens more suffered serious burns and broken limbs. The survivors walked out, were thrown out, or jumped out. Many bore permanent physical scars; all bore deep emotional wounds. Of the ten or more students (no one knows exactly how many) that Lieutenant Charles Kamin saved by throwing them out the window, all survived.

Word of the disaster spread around the world. In Rome, Pope John XXIII sent a personal message of condolence and solace to the archbishop of Chicago, the Most Reverend Albert Gregory Meyer. Four days after the tragedy, the archbishop conducted a mass for the victims and their families in front of an altar set up in an armory. The fire, he said solemnly, was "a great and inescapable sorrow."

Even experienced firefighters, who dealt with death many times, could never put this tragedy behind them. To the day he died thirty-four years later, Kamin admitted he could still hear the haunting screams of the burning children of Room 211.

If there was any consolation to those who lost a loved one in this heartrending catastrophe, it came in the belief that the victims didn't die in vain. That's because the fire prompted revisions in school safety codes and increased enforcement of existing codes across the country. Cities and towns launched major inspections of all their schools. Where necessary, new laws were passed making it mandatory that schools have enclosed stairwells, fire doors, sprinkler systems, and alarm systems connected to the fire department. The tragedy of the Our Lady of Angels fire has since saved an untold number lives.

EYE OF THE FIRESTORM

Veteran firefighters Vinnie Bollon and Charlie Radtke were chewing fast, hoping to finish lunch before the next fire call sounded. But there was no such luck on this hectic day.

The next alarm sounded halfway through lunch. "Damn, not again," Radtke complained. He hurriedly swallowed a couple of gulps of food, grabbed his gear, and sprinted for the silver pole down to their engine.

The Ladder 31 firehouse, called "La Casa Grande" by its South Bronx neighbors, was just two blocks away from Fort Apache, the New York Police Department's notorious Four-One Precinct that was made famous in movies and books as the toughest cop turf on Earth.

Ladder 31 was the busiest fire company in the world, answering nearly ten thousand fire alarms a year or about twenty-eight a day, from little blazes that could be quickly snuffed out with an extinguisher to monster conflagrations that could take down an entire block. Especially vulnerable in the older parts of the neighborhood were the dilapidated wood-frame apartment buildings, many of which had been abandoned when residents fled to the suburbs.

Already on that July morning in 1978, Bollon and his partner had been on a half-dozen runs and they were both tired, their eyes stinging, their muscles sore. "It's been nonstop fire calls," Bollon grumbled to Radtke.

Leaving a big piece of sandwich behind and wishing he had time to get a cold beer, Bollon wrapped himself around the pole a split second behind Radtke.

"Here we go again!" Radtke yelled as they barreled out of the red brick house, horn and siren cutting through the thick, humid summer air. They roared off toward a six-story, H-shaped apartment building. The fire had erupted across the street from one of the battered buildings where President Jimmy Carter had stood a year earlier and promised the United States he would rebuild the South Bronx and reclaim America's cities. But long after the president returned to the White House, the Bronx continued to burn.

Eye of the Firestorm

The fire truck raced through the crowded streets, dodging around double-parked cars, boys playing stickball, and girls jumping rope.

"Let it be an easy one, please, Lord," Bollon prayed.

But it didn't look like his prayer would be answered. Flames were shooting out of the windows on the fourth floor, a tip-off to the two veteran smoke-eaters that they could be in for a hard time. What concerned them the most was that the building was home to dozens of people. The firefighters feared that some of them might be trapped behind the wall of flames.

When the truck arrived, worried residents stood in front of the building, gaping up at the black smoke and orange flames. Most of the women were in housedresses, a few clutched pet cats, and some were holding on to their prized possessions.

As the firemen dragged hoses up to the building, an "additional information" bulletin call came over the rig's radio: "Report residents still on floors above the fire."

"We gotta get 'em out," Radtke hollered to his partner.

As the "forceable entry team" for this fire, it was the duo's duty to get everyone out of the building. Other firemen would wield the hoses to fight the blaze. Bollon and Radtke needed to go to the floor above the fire and search every apartment to make sure nobody was inside. If they found anyone, the next and hardest step would be getting them past the flames and smoke coming from the floor below. In past fires, the two firemen often found themselves struggling with the people they were trying to save because blind fear of burning to death in flames robbed the victims of their good sense or left them too paralyzed to move.

Bollon grabbed his axe and Halligan, a big steel pry bar good for popping open locked doors and cracking open walls. Radtke put a big fist around a six-foot wood pike, a kind of medieval-looking spear with a hook on the end. It's an essential tool for pulling down walls and exposing the fire.

"This is it, brother," Bollon yelled as he and Radtke began their dash up the emergency stairs.

When they charged past the fire floor and hadn't encountered any residents, Radtke said, "Maybe they all got out." Deep down he knew that wasn't likely.

"There were a lot of people outside," Bollon replied, knowing that it was probably wishful thinking that the building was now empty.

Once above the fire, the two men hurried into a smoke-filled hallway on the fifth floor. "Look at that. The doors are open," said Bollon, scanning the row of apartment doors. That probably meant the tenants had run for their lives and were safely out on the street. But the two firemen still had to check each apartment, just on the off chance that someone was still inside.

"Nobody home," Radtke announced almost jubilantly as he checked out the first few apartments.

"Maybe we got lucky. Maybe they're all at Yankee Stadium," Bollon said as he exited one empty apartment and entered another one.

Then their luck ran out. The door to one of the apartments was shut tight. Radtke tried to turn the knob. "It's locked." They both knew that meant there was a strong likelihood that someone was still inside, perhaps cowering in a closet or in a bathtub or too disabled or scared to move.

"Okay, let's pop it," Bollon said.

"Don't let it be a kid trapped inside," Radtke said as he braced his feet and swung the axe. Bollon jammed the pry bar into the tiny crack between the door and the frame. In seconds, the lock broke with a twang and the wood cracked as the door was pried off its hinges.

"No welcome mat," Bollon joked as they peered into the entry foyer. Swirls of dense smoke curled up around tongues of flickering flames from under the doors of the two closets to the left. "The fire is coming up from below through the closet," observed Bollon.

"There's probably someone in there, someone scared to death," said Radtke, remembering the hundreds of people he'd rescued from burning buildings in his more than ten years on the job.

His arm still ached when it rained, a painful reminder of the broken arm he had suffered in a rescue a year earlier. He had gone into a burning building just like this one and encountered a woman who was overweight, mad with fear, and spoke only Spanish. Try as he might, he couldn't convince her it was safe to take the stairs. Instead, she knocked him out of the way and climbed out the window and onto the fire escape. Radtke had no choice but to go with her and guide her down the ladder without killing herself. The fire escape was old and rusty and, because of their combined weight, it pulled away from the building, sending Radtke and the woman plunging twenty feet to the ground. She landed on top of him, breaking his arm. He cushioned her fall, but she still lost an eye when her head hit the edge of the fire escape on the way down.

Radtke glanced at Bollon and could tell by the look in his face that he too was probably reliving a similar rescue attempt. All firefighters had them.

Both dropped to their bellies at the same time. This wasn't a new routine. The two men had worked side by side for years and moved together like the Radio City Rockettes. Both of them put their noses down to the linoleum and crawled under the acrid, stinging smoke. They were groping blindly until they got to the end of the foyer and could start to see again.

They searched the kitchen and bathroom, but no one was there. "Hey," Bollon yelled to Radtke. "There's a woman in the bedroom."

Sitting in an upholstered chair, one hand over her face to hide her eyes, was a 50-something woman wearing an ordinary housedress. She didn't utter a sound even after two men in helmets and turnout coats had just busted into her apartment. They both thought she looked odd. She was clearly upset, but didn't appear frightened at all.

"Hey, lady, you can't stay here," Bollon told her. "The building is on fire."

But the woman didn't respond.

"Maybe she's been burned," Radtke whispered to his partner. "That could be why she's covering her face."

"Well, we better get her out of here fast."

Bollon and Radtke both had the same thought: She had given up on escaping through the burning hallway and was just sitting there waiting for the fire to take her life.

Bollon put a hand on her shoulder and said, "You're going to be all right now. We'll get you out. You're going to be safe." He repeated the comforting words over and over in an effort to make her believe they had everything under control.

"Don't worry," Radtke told her in his most soothing, confident voice. Over the years, he had learned to be a good actor.

The fire was bad, but it wasn't totally out of control. Firefighters from other units had put their hoses in action and were starting to hold their own against the flames. But the blaze had already spread from the fourth floor to the two upper stories.

For a few moments it looked like a routine rescue for the two firefighters.

Then Bollon gently tried to take the woman's arm to lead her to safety. But she shook him off angrily and started to wail. "I don't want to leave," she cried. "I'm not going. I can't go outside."

"Sure you can," Radtke said softly as he reached for her right arm while Bollon clutched her left arm.

"Lady, you're not staying here," Bollon said sternly. "You're coming with us."

She resisted but she was no match for the two burly firefighters who wrestled her toward the hallway. By this time more flames were licking out of the closets and the smoke was getting thicker, so Bollon and Radtke forced the struggling woman to the floor. While one pushed her, the other pulled her across the floor past the flames and under the smoke. They both took turns to make sure she kept her head down near the floor where the air was cooler and still breathable.

In about a minute they had removed the reluctant resident from her apartment and into the hallway where the smoke was less thick. Bollon handed her off to Radtke.

"I'll get her down," said Radtke. He left his partner momentarily to guide the woman down the stairs past the fire to the second-floor landing. Pointing toward the door on the floor below, he told her, "Okay, there's the exit. You'll be safe now." He waited until she headed down the steps before he turned around and bounded back up to rejoin his partner.

"Mission accomplished," he told Bollon, who still was checking apartments on the fifth floor. "Anybody else inside?"

"Nope," Bollon replied. "So far, all are empty. Not even a goldfish left behind."

After a couple of minutes, the two sweat-drenched men had looked into most of the apartments on the fifth floor. They were beginning to relax a little, relieved that there had been only one person in danger, and that person was out of harm's way.

Suddenly they heard a voice coming from the emergency stairway. An elderly man, who had lingered on the building's top floor and had only now decided to evacuate, shouted to them through the exit. "I think I just saw a lady go in her apartment!" Then he continued down the exit stairs.

"Where? Who?" Bollon called after him.

"Don't know. It was a lady," the man yelled back, never breaking his stride. "She had her hand over her face."

Both firefighters stared at each other in disbelief, then looked toward the door that they had forced open just minutes earlier. Despite its broken lock and busted hinges, the door was closed.

"What the hell is that stupid woman doing?" Radtke growled, angry that he would have to go inside, get down on the floor, and drag her out again. "I'll take this," he told Bollon. "You finish up."

So while Bollon headed for the last few apartments on the far end of the floor, Radtke entered the burning apartment a second time. He went nose to the floor, under the flames and smoke in the hallway and crawled into the kitchen and bathroom, which were empty. In the bedroom, he spotted the woman in the housedress with her arm over her face. She was sitting in her chair right where she had been the first time. *This is déjà vu all over again,* he thought.

He was through being nice to her; obviously, that approach didn't work the first time. So Radtke was much more harsh now. "Lady, the building is burning. Don't you understand? You can't stay here."

Eye of the Firestorm

He grasped her left arm and yanked her toward the hall. As in the first rescue, she kept hiding her face from him with her right hand. This time she didn't say a word. But she still put up a struggle.

Why is she doing this? he wondered. *What is going through her head?*

"Look, lady, I don't know why you're resisting but you're not staying here, not with this fire. Don't you realize you could die?"

In frustration, Radtke was forced to shove the uncooperative fire victim into the foyer of her apartment. For the second time he pushed her down to the floor and then hauled her out past the flames. "No, no!" she cried. "Don't do this! I don't want to go out there!"

Without bothering Bollon, who was still going through other apartments, Radtke half carried, half pushed the protesting woman out the door. "I can't go outside!" she whined. "I won't go so please don't make me!" Radtke ignored her pleas and kept pushing her from behind in the corridor toward the stairs.

From the far end of the hall, Bollon popped out of an apartment in time to see his partner forcing the woman to the stairs. *My God, this is just like the "Twilight Zone,"* Bollon thought. But it wasn't anything like a TV drama for Radtke. It was just extra work and extra danger in real life with a real fire.

She obviously has no clue to the danger she's put

herself and me in, Radtke told himself. *If she keeps this up, she's going to get me killed.*

This time he escorted her all the way down the stairs and out the door where he left her near one of the fire rigs. "Now don't move!" he ordered.

Turning to some nearby policemen and firefighters, he said, "Will somebody please make sure she stays here?" Without waiting for an answer, Radtke dashed back toward the burning building to give Bollon a hand in finishing up the search. He didn't like leaving his partner alone in a blaze. That's the way firefighters get killed.

"You meet a lot of nuts," Radtke muttered to himself as he headed away from the woman who was still covering her face.

When he reached Bollon and told him the story of the repeat rescue, they shook their heads and returned to the task of making sure nobody was left in danger. They didn't give another thought to the woman.

That is, until Bollon saw the shadowy figure of a person through the smoke in the hallway. He couldn't be sure but it looked like someone had gone into an apartment—the very same woman's apartment. "Oh, damn it. Not again," Bollon groaned.

"What are you talking about?" Radtke asked.

"Your lady friend just returned again."

For the third time, Radtke went back into the

apartment, slipped under the smoke, and dodged the flames. He didn't bother to look in the kitchen or the bathroom, but hurried into the bedroom. Just as he expected, she was sitting in her chair with her hand over her face, the same as the first two times. She was paying no mind to the smoke and soot that were blanketing everything in the room.

Radtke knew that within minutes, the thickening smoke and soot could fill her lungs and suffocate her if she remained in the apartment.

"That hand over your face isn't going to help you," he said. "Lady, you can't stay here. I keep telling you that. If you do, you'll die in here."

"I can't go out," she mumbled in a voice filled with despair. "I can't let people see me like this."

"Why the hell not? The building is on fire. Nobody cares what you look like at a time like this."

He tried to haul her out of the chair, but she resisted. He was ready to club her unconscious if necessary to save her life and his. He had a job to do, maybe other lives to save, and she was getting in his way.

"My eye," she wailed. "I can't find my eye."

"What are you talking about?"

She dropped the hand that had been covering her face and showed Radtke what she was hiding. Where her left eye should have been was nothing but a crater.

"Nobody knows that I wear a glass eye," she explained. "Before the building caught fire, I popped it out and took a nap. When I woke up to all the commotion from the fire, I couldn't remember where I had left my eye." Her lips began to quiver and her voice broke. "I can't let people see me without my eye."

Radtke didn't know what to do. Sure, there were flames and smoke all around. Sure, it made more sense to drag her out right this second. But he realized if he did that, he'd be back in this apartment a fourth time, towing this crazy woman out again.

"Okay, okay," Radtke said with a sigh. "I'll look for it." He searched the soot-covered chest of drawers, the nightstand and the floor next to the bed. Nothing

All the while, the woman cried softly, "They can't see me without my eye." She kept repeating the words as if the more times she said it, the better the fireman would understand her plight.

Radtke hurriedly rifled through a couple of other drawers and finally gave up when the smoke made it hard to breathe. "I can't look anymore," he snapped. "We're leaving this instant!"

Radtke started to grab her for the third time when he spotted a marble-like lump covered with soot near the threshold of the bedroom door. He walked over and picked it up. "Is this it?" he asked

The woman, who had been watching him like a

hawk with her good eye, lunged like a cat and grabbed the precious hunk of glass out of his hand. "Yes! Yes!" she squealed with relief. She wiped the soot off the glass eye with the bedspread and then popped it into her empty socket. "Can we go now?" Radtke asked.

She nodded her head. This time Radtke didn't have to wrestle her to the floor when they reached the burning entry foyer. She got down on the floor and let him guide her under the smoke. She acted like a pro who had done it all before, which she had. Then she headed down the stairs and out of the building as quick as her legs would carry her.

When Radtke rejoined his partner and told him what happened, Bollon slapped him on the back and said, "Good job. She's finally happy. She has her eye and now she can face her neighbors." He paused and added, "By the way, Radtke, what is it with you and one-eyed women?"

AT ROPE'S END

Atlanta firefighter Matt Moseley of Squad 4 didn't think much of the white smoke billowing across Interstate I-75 on his way to battle a blaze in an area known as Cabbagetown on the sunny, windy afternoon of April 12, 1999.

Aww, it's probably nothing, just leaves or trash, he thought. *It'll burn itself out.* So, as the big truck from the city's Heavy Rescue Company barreled along, Moseley began planning the dinner he intended to fix back at the station.

But the burly thirty-year-old smoke-eater never made that dinner. Before the day was through, his life and that of a forty-nine-year-old crane operator would be dangling by a thread—actually, an eighty-foot rope lashed to a helicopter hovering over an inferno.

The fire truck rolled up to the scene of the fire, which wasn't burning trash but rather a burning building: the old Fulton Bag and Cotton Mill, a six-story, century-old, brick-and-wood-beam warehouse. It was the place where tarps for the fire department had been made years ago. Now the old building was being renovated into loft apartments.

Moseley and fourteen other firefighters, each carrying a high-rise pack—a rolled-up hose and a coupler that can connect with another hose—dashed into the building as construction workers calmly filed out.

"Be careful, some of those floor beams are rotten and the flooring is full of holes," one worker told the firemen as he left the building.

Seeing little smoke inside, none of the firefighters put on masks. Because all of the old windows had been removed during the renovation, 40 mph wind gusts had blown the smoke out of the building. It was the same wind that had nearly wrecked Moseley's barbecue dinner party the night before, so having gusts that blew away the smoke evened the score for Moseley.

The firefighters ran up the stairs to the empty, cavernous fourth floor, where they found a thirty-by forty-foot patch of flames surrounded by several spent fire extinguishers. The workers had tried to snuff out the fire themselves, but only managed to exacerbate the situation by delaying a call to 911.

The firemen needed to pump water up because

there were no standpipes or sprinklers. Within minutes, ladders fitted with hoses were placed on the side of the building. Firefighters inside began attaching the ladder hoses to the hoses from their high-rise packs.

The firemen on the fourth floor were in the middle of coupling the hoses when they realized the blaze was spreading. Flames were shooting out of the elevator shaft.

"Look up there!" Moseley shouted, pointing to the ceiling. Flames were breaking through the slats of the floor above them.

"Get someone and go and see what's happening up there!" a commander ordered.

Moseley and Lieutenant Mark Green from another company raced up the stairs to investigate. They encountered a fire on the upper floor that looked as if it would be easy to snuff out. But then all of a sudden, Moseley and Green were engulfed in dense, black smoke that billowed around their waists. The flames grew in intensity.

"We better get water or we better get out!" Moseley shouted. Without more hands, it would be foolhardy to try to tackle the fire alone. They started back down toward the fourth floor when the smoldering fire on the fifth floor burst into an inferno.

From the outside they heard the voice of a battalion chief bellow, "Get out of there! Everybody out!"

Firefighters started bounding down the stairs as Moseley heard the whoosh from the wind blowing through the windowless building and the snap, snap, snap of the floor beams falling.

The building had been designed so that in a fire the beams would collapse but the walls would stay intact, making it easy to rebuild. Over the years, the twelve- by twelve-inch timbers had dried and absorbed oils and fibers from the cotton that had been made into cloth at the old mill. Now the timbers were ablaze as if they had been soaked in kerosene.

There was no way to fight the fire from inside. Retreat was the only alternative.

Moseley suddenly remembered he had left some tools on the other side of the fifth floor. "I gotta go get those tools I left over there," he yelled to Ed Hill, another rescue squad firefighter.

"You better leave those tools right where they are," Hill barked. "They're not worth collecting life insurance for. Get out. Now!"

As Moseley scampered down the stairs, he kept glancing behind him. By the time he had cleared the second floor, he saw a black column of smoke billow into flames that were licking at the boots of two officers who were trailing him.

I'm gonna die in here, Moseley said to himself, oddly calm about facing what he thought was his impending doom. *So this is how it's gonna end.*

At Rope's End

But he wasn't giving up. He kept pounding down the stairs and then made a mad dash through an exit door. When he was safely outside, Moseley looked up to see smoke coming out of every window.

All the firefighters who had been inside were accounted for except for Lieutenant Mark Green who had been with Moseley on the fifth floor. Moseley went back in through a different door to look for him, but Moseley could get no further than the third-floor landing before a hail of tumbling red-hot flaming bricks forced him back outside.

Out in the open again, Moseley was relieved to hear over the two-way radio that the missing officer had made it out. The lieutenant had rushed down the stairs and raced off in another direction to his fire truck, which was melting from the heat of the fire. Green hopped in the cab of his rig and moved it to safety. Meanwhile, all the fire engines were being pulled back in full retreat as the blaze and heat threatened to destroy anything nearby. (One fireman who had left his shoes on a rescue truck returned to find they had been melted by the intense heat.)

Moseley had never seen anything like this in the seven years he had been fighting blazes. Now he knew what a firestorm felt like.

"We'll have to make an exterior attack," Captain Tom Doyle told his men. The firefighters were aiming heavy-caliber streams of water at the flames, which were shooting out of the mill's windows. Soon about 150 firefighters were called in to battle the seven-alarm blaze.

After Squad 4 moved its trucks away from the heat, Moseley and his colleagues ran to the nearby wood-frame apartments that were in danger of catching fire from the falling embers of the mill. The firemen ordered an immediate evacuation. Although most of the residents were at work, the firefighters were busy breaking into apartments to rescue pet dogs, cats, and even goldfish. While Moseley was gathering residents to watch over the pets, strong gusts had fanned the flames, turning the old cotton mill into one white-hot mass.

Moseley and the other members of Squad 4 were catching their breath when a crackly voice came over their radio: "We have a rope rescue. Get back to the truck."

"Oh, great," groaned one of the men, "we're going to have to leave this fire probably to save some window washer downtown."

As the members of Rescue 4 jogged back to their truck, Moseley noticed a small crowd of firefighters, construction workers, and reporters gawking at something above the fire. So he looked too.

Moseley spotted a man's head peeking over the side of the control cab of a tower crane about 250 feet above the ground, next to the burning building. The crane had been used to haul material for the renovation. Nobody realized that when the fire broke out, the crane operator—forty-nine-year-old Ivers Sims of Woodland, Alabama—was still up in the cab. Now he was trapped.

When the flames and heat had blocked his way down, Sims had decided to patiently wait for Atlanta's bravest to extinguish the fire. But then the fire turned into an inferno. Sims remained in the control cab as long as he could, talking to his supervisor on the ground via radio, until it got too hot to stay. When the soles of his shoes started to melt, he left the cab and carefully walked over the searing-hot steelwork to the eight-foot-thick concrete counterweights on the far end of the crane's boom where the heat was less searing. He laid down flat on his belly, literally cooling his heels.

Sims planted himself there, hoping rescuers would either get him off or extinguish the fire before the steel got too hot and the crane bent like a wax candle. Several news helicopters buzzed overhead. One tried to get close enough for him to hop aboard its runner, but the scorching updraft forced it to back off.

On the ground, the spreading flames had engulfed the nearby apartments. *At least we got the animals out,* Moseley thought. Then he turned his attention to the man stranded on the crane's concrete counterweights.

"Holy cow," Moseley said to his colleagues. "How are we gonna get this guy down with the whole east end burning like this?"

Not sure what they were going to do, Moseley and firefighter Bill Bowes quickly unloaded rescue equipment, including ropes and descent-control devices, and strapped themselves into harnesses.

"What are we gonna do, shoot him a rope?" Moseley asked.

"Think we can throw it to him from another building?" Bowes replied.

"Not unless a guy shows up wearing a big red cape with an 'S' on it."

Captain Doyle was on the radio, seeking a clearance for a rescue attempt. "Chief, if we can get a helicopter, we can get a man to rappel down to him."

"No," the chief responded. "It's too dangerous."

Now the steel on the crane was turning black, a sign that the temperatures were reaching a steel-softening 1,100 degrees. Soon the melting crane would begin to lean over, throwing the trapped operator to his death.

The situation was desperate and the fire officials knew it. They had to do something. They couldn't just stand there and watch a man die a gruesome death.

At Rope's End

Moseley was standing directly behind Captain Doyle when the chief, over the radio, reversed his own decision and ordered a risky helicopter rescue. They would attempt to lower a firefighter from a rope and snatch the stranded man from the crane. What made this attempt so dicey was that no Atlanta rescue team had ever done or even trained for this procedure. Adding to the difficulty were the strong, tricky winds.

Overhearing the radio conversation between the captain and the chief was exciting and fascinating for Moseley, who couldn't wait to see how this rescue would be pulled off. He knew it was a desperate plan that required someone with skill and nerves of steel, a real-life Superman.

As he eavesdropped over the captain's shoulder, Moseley heard the call go out for a helicopter—any kind of chopper. Then Captain Doyle whirled around, stared straight into Moseley's pale blue eyes, and announced, "You're going."

Moseley hadn't given any thought that he might be the one who was picked. He was tempted to look around on the off chance the captain had picked someone else, but the firefighter knew he had been tapped for the dangerous assignment. All he could do was gulp and rub his now shaky hands through his blond crew cut. Moseley, who had no training with helicopters, figured the only reason he was picked was that his was the first face the captain saw when he turned around.

This would be suicide, Moseley thought. Terrified, he tried to swallow but couldn't. His mouth went dry. "Can somebody get me some water?" he asked no one in particular. His mind whirled with thoughts of self-doubt. *Should I back out of this? Should I say, "No way?" Sure, but if I'm gonna say that, I better get into another business because my business is being a firefighter.*

Moments later a Bell Ranger traffic copter on loan from a local news station touched down in the nearest landing zone, next to an old cemetery. *That's kind of fitting,* Moseley thought, *a graveyard.*

Moseley, fellow firefighters Bill Bowes and Ed Hill, Captain Doyle, and the pilot huddled together to conjure up a workable plan.

"How about tying me onto a landing strut?" Moseley asked the pilot.

"I wouldn't do that," came the reply.

The solution, they decided, was to have Bowes strap himself into a seat and lower Moseley, who would be in a harness, out of the chopper on a rescue rope. Bowes would have the rope clipped to his body harness and threaded through a break bar rack, a washboard-like contraption of steel pipes used for rescues. The rack would control tension on the rope and allow Bowes to play it out in a slow controlled manner once Moseley started his descent.

"I'll be the dope on the rope," Moseley joked. "Bill, I know you can lower me, but when I get the other guy, can you handle both our weights?"

"Well, if I can't, I'll go down with you," Bowes replied in his best John Wayne imitation.

"Hey, Bill," Moseley said, "this is no time for bad movie quotes."

It was decided that Hill would lash himself to another seat and prop his feet against the aircraft's bulkhead while bracing Bowes.

This is beginning to sound like Moe, Larry, and Curly, Moseley said to himself. But he was resigned to his fate and was determined to do his best to make the crazy plan work. He tried to swallow but couldn't. *Where is that drink of water?*

Moseley gazed at Hill and Bowes. He could tell from the look in their eyes that they were leery about the plan. It seemed like a suicide mission, but there was no choice. They couldn't let this man die.

The trio was boarding the traffic copter when Moseley spotted another chopper coming in for a landing. It was from the Georgia Department of Natural Resources, and was rigged up for fighting forest fires and for conducting mountain rescues. It arrived just in time.

"That's what we need!" Moseley shouted to the

others. He unhooked himself from the seat of the traffic copter and raced over to the other chopper.

After exchanging introductions with crew chief Larry Rogers and pilot Boyd Clines, Moseley felt relieved when he learned that they were experienced in attempting delicate and dangerous rescues.

Rogers got down to business right away and instructed Moseley on how to rescue the crane operator. "If the trapped guy is panicked or if he's too nervous, we will lower a basket," he explained. "The basket has a steel frame stretcher and you'll have to strap him in. If the guy is really jittery, you'll have to strap yourself in with him, and you'll go up together."

At this point the cold terror that had gripped Moseley when he was tapped for the rescue assignment began to ease. He pictured himself being lowered out of the chopper on a winched rope, snatching the man and then being brought back safely into the helicopter to complete a flawless mission.

Moseley was pumped. He was psyched. He was ready to go.

With renewed confidence, he hopped into the helicopter only to see Rogers outside, shaking his head and motioning him to step out. "Come with me," Rogers ordered.

Puzzled, Moseley followed Rogers to a spot several yards in front of the chopper. Then he looked down and saw eighty feet of rope snaking out from the bottom of the craft and hooked to a "D" ring. Rogers walked with him to the end of the rope. Pointing to a spot on Moseley's harness, Rogers said, "Hook the rope right here and we'll take care of the rest."

Moseley realized he wasn't going to be lowered from the chopper. He was going to be dangling from it throughout the entire mission. The fear that had left his body moments earlier came rushing back like a tidal wave.

Rogers calmly explained. "The bird goes up slow and steady. As it does, you walk toward the helicopter and we'll take up the slack slowly. Remember to walk directly toward the ship, and then get directly under it."

"Okay," Moseley said, trying hard to pretend this would be a piece of cake.

Moseley knew those would be the last words they would exchange until the end of the mission, because the fire department's radios and the state's radios were not compatible. He would not be able to talk to the pilot.

Moseley clutched a twenty-foot piece of nylon webbing and some metal clips on his harness. It was for making a "quick tie" that would attach Sims to him and allow him to lift the trapped man off his perch.

Don't drop this webbing, don't drop this webbing, he told himself. Those words ran through his head like an annoying advertising jingle. Seconds later, the chopper lifted off. He moved under the gradually rising helicopter until he felt his harness tighten and his feet leave the ground.

To his surprise, the higher he rose, the lower the fear factor. He was absolutely calm. *What a beautiful day it is,* he said to himself as he dangled eighty feet below the chopper. He looked down and saw that the blaze had spread to several houses. *Wow, what a fire. For a fireman this is some sight.*

Then a fatalistic thought crossed his mind. *If you're a fireman, this is the way to go. This is a good day to die.* "This is right out of a bad movie," he said out loud and then began to laugh.

The chopper flew toward the stranded man, moving slowly to keep Moseley below it and not trailing behind it like a water skier being towed by a speedboat.

As the helicopter flew directly over the burning building, he gazed down at the fiery black shell and thought, *This is like looking into hell.* Even from this height, he could feel the hot air from the flames. *I hope he doesn't stop here. If he does I'll be cooked.*

As they flew closer to the crane, Moseley felt little stings, the first signs that his skin was beginning to burn from the heat of the fire below. He covered his face with the collar of his turnout coat, wishing this rescue would go faster.

Moseley forgot about the fire when he saw the stranded operator sitting with his legs hanging off the concrete counterweight.

"Don't panic," Moseley yelled at Sims. "Don't grab for me. I'll do it all. Just stay put." As the chopper moved in, Moseley found himself rotating on the rope so his back was toward the crane. Try as he might, he couldn't get himself turned around to face Sims.

I gotta turn, I gotta turn. I'm never going to be able to do this if I can't turn, Moseley thought, trying not to get too flustered. Suddenly, through no doing of his own, he turned 180 degrees until he was facing Sims. *God, you must have done that,* he said to himself. *Thanks, God.*

When the helicopter hovered low near Sims to give the firefighter plenty of slack on his rope, Moseley grabbed a guy wire on the crane and pulled himself onto the steel deck.

"Watch out. There are holes," Sims warned. As Moseley headed toward the stranded operator, the fireman looked down and noticed he was following black footprints on the crane's deck. He realized they were the footprints left by the operator's melting shoes.

Trying to break the tension of the situation and to relax Sims, Moseley quipped, "Hey, your boss sent me up to tell you that you can knock off early today."

Sims just looked at him without saying a word. It was hard for Moseley to tell if Sims was too scared or too cool to laugh.

Okay, no more jokes, Moseley told himself. *Let's stick with the basics.* He immediately wrapped Sims in a "quick tie" harness, made from the webbing he had been clutching to his chest. He fastened on one metal clip and then used a second clip to attach Sims to his own body harness.

Through it all Sims didn't say a word.

Not big on the chitchat, Moseley thought. When Sims was secured to Moseley, the firefighter gave a thumbs up—the sign to the pilot to lift the two men off the crane. Within seconds, Sims and Moseley were whisked away.

Not one word was spoken during the two minutes it took for the chopper to bring the men safely to the landing zone where jubilant firefighters rushed toward them and unhooked the rope from the harness.

Fellow firefighters cheered and slapped Moseley on the back. He could hardly talk because his mouth, which had been parched before takeoff, now felt like he had swallowed the Sahara. Someone offered him a cup of water, but Moseley's hand was shaking so badly he couldn't get his gloves off. A colleague helped him remove the gloves and then handed him a cup. But Moseley's hands were still trembling, causing him to spill half the water.

Oddly, Sims was much calmer. When the firefighters wanted to carry him on a stretcher to a waiting ambulance, he smiled and said, "I'm fine. I can walk there." Sims was treated at Atlanta Medical Center for smoke inhalation and exposure to high heat, but otherwise was uninjured.

Moseley hustled over to the helicopter, smiled at Clines and Rogers, and told them, "The first round is on me."

A few minutes later, the radio crackled, and the men of Rescue 4 were off to battle another fire. In fact, they handled two more small ones later that day and returned to the firehouse about midnight.

Moseley thought he would fall to sleep right away, but he tossed all night. Somewhere around dawn, he dozed off for about thirty minutes. When he looked outside the next morning, he saw that the street in front of the firehouse was teeming with TV satellite trucks and reporters all waiting to talk to him.

Interviews went on throughout the morning. On ABC's *Good Morning America,* Sims, from the hospital, sent a message to Moseley, "Thank you, Matt. Thank God for your courage and bravery. I'm going to change your name to Moses, not Moseley."

Later in the day, Moseley met with Georgia Governor Roy Barnes, who issued a proclamation praising his courage. Moseley's twenty-four-hour shift had stretched into a thirty-five-hour day, but he still couldn't sleep that night, opting instead to attend a party. He was running on pure adrenaline.

State officials scrambled to be seen in public with him, including Atlanta Mayor Bill Campbell, who had been feuding with the firefighters' union for years. The union was seeking new safety equipment, especially replacements for defective breathing masks, and a raise, including a $2,000 bonus, but their requests went unheeded.

Union leaders were incensed when the mayor showed up on a national TV morning show, lauding Moseley's heroics. Moseley, a union man himself, decided that he would put his fifteen minutes of fame to good use by confronting Campbell.

Moseley and the mayor met in the bunk room of the firehouse alone. Knowing that the street was still jammed with satellite trucks, Moseley told him, "We can go out in front of the media where I will bring up the needs of the firefighters or we can meet now and come to some kind of peace."

Campbell gave in. It took forty-five minutes to break through an eight-year impasse. The mayor agreed to spend $1.2 million on air packs, start a program to replace old fire engines, and buy other needed modern equipment. At the end of the meeting, an aide for the mayor came in and reminded Campbell that the city budget couldn't afford the fire department's needs. Campbell cut him short.

"Just do it," the mayor ordered. Then he looked at Moseley and said, "I guess you want the $2,000 bonus, too." Moseley didn't expect it. But he took it. So did every other firefighter in the Atlanta Fire Department.

RUINS
OF
HORROR

Dragging himself through the tight dark passage in the rubble of broken concrete and twisted steel, Doug Jewett could smell death. It was the stench of dozens of bodies rotting in the ruins of what had been one of Mexico City's top hospitals.

He froze as an aftershock from the killer earthquake that had leveled much of the city sent chunks of concrete bouncing off his hardhat. *The next one could be the one that crushes me,* the forty-two-year-old firefighter said to himself as dust filled his nostrils and stung his eyes. Four to five tremors an hour kept rocking the area, making the unstable rubble even more treacherous. Despite a perilous job that for days now had put him in constant jeopardy of becoming a casualty himself, he continued searching for victims who might still be clinging to life under the wreckage.

Jewett couldn't quit now, especially when he

knew that somewhere deep in the debris of the demolished hospital, helpless newborns were still alive. He could hear their weakening whimpers. So he pressed on, squeezing and squirming through the stinking, grimy ruins and past the mangled corpses that created a grotesque, ungodly world bordering on the surreal.

Suddenly Jewett came across a live, barely conscious newborn. But the rescuer's excitement over the discovery was tempered by the realization that the baby's tiny right leg was crushed and trapped under a hunk of concrete. Jewett studied the dire situation. *The concrete is impossible to move. His little leg has been crushed for days and no doctor on God's green earth can save it.* He gazed at the fragile baby boy. *There's no way I can get him out with his leg intact, and there's no way I'm going to leave him here to die. Damn, I've got only one option.*

Jewett took out his large razor-sharp Rambo knife and whispered to the infant, "I'm sorry I have to do this to you, little guy." Then Jewett cut off the baby's leg.

It was just one of many hard choices that Jewett had had to make ever since he arrived after a massive earthquake—8.1 on the Richter scale—hit Mexico City on September 19, 1985. An aftershock a day later reached 7.1, reducing sections of the vibrant city of eighteen million to a pile of burning debris, dead bodies, and lost souls. The tremor was so powerful it had leveled much of the capital and devastated eight states in Mexico.

The quake left more than four hundred thousand homeless, killed at least ten thousand people, seriously injured tens of thousands more, and destroyed more than five thousand buildings, including twenty-seven hospitals and forty-eight schools. Trapped inside those collapsed structures were thousands of people who survived the initial tremor but now faced an agonizing death by being either slowly crushed by shifting rubble or being burned alive.

Rescue teams from all over the world flew in to help find survivors. Jewett, chief of the Urban Rescue and Recovery Squad of the Miami Dade Fire Rescue Department in Florida, was a veteran lifesaver who had seen it all since joining the department in 1963—earthquakes in Venezuela, floods in Honduras, and hurricanes in Florida. As soon as he heard the news on the radio of the earthquake, he began packing his bags.

The Mexican government hadn't asked for outside rescue workers. Instead, it wanted high-tech equipment, like the Jaws of Life, and three thousand self-contained breathing units. Within hours after the tremor struck, the United States State Department phoned Jewett, primarily to find out where it could get the equipment.

Jewett, who also was a rescue trainer for the State Department, strongly believed that in unskilled hands this gear could do more harm than good. He had been summoned before to help in other Latin American disasters, so he knew there would be a lack of trained rescue people there. "It'll be a lot better if I go down with one of my men and survey the scene," he told the State Department.

After some haggling with Washington officials, who didn't want to rile the Mexican government, Jewett and another Miami rescue expert, Jimmy Arias, were given the green light to help out. The two firefighters hooked up with six Army demolition specialists and hopped a flight to Mexico City.

When the plane flew over the devastation, Jewett looked out the window at the hellish scene below of collapsed buildings and roaring fires. "Boy, have we got work to do," he told Arias. "I just know there are plenty of people still alive in those buildings."

Jewett's experience taught him to read rubble like some people read newspapers. One look at the destruction told him there were plenty of "voids"— small air pockets and open places in debris where survivors can live for days. The city was sitting on an old lakebed, so when the buildings fell, they slid sideways, a perfect condition for the formation of lifesaving voids.

But to reach those voids, rescuers would have to

move tens of thousands of pounds of concrete as carefully as if they were children playing a game of pickup sticks. It was the kind of painstaking work that took hours to move inches of rubble and often days to reach just one survivor. And that was only if the operation was handled by experienced rescuers.

Mexican officials were not cooperative. They had already brought in the military and were bulldozing debris, dynamiting weakened structures, and fumigating the ruins to kill off rats, even though such actions could kill hundreds of survivors still trapped underneath. No amount of arguing or pleading from international rescuers could get the Mexicans to stop.

Frustrated, the Miami firefighter went straight to the United States Embassy, hoping to initiate a rescue operation. Instead, at the request of the Mexican government, he and Arias were sent to its naval headquarters, where they were asked to probe through the debris for the only copy of the military's disaster plan for the city.

Jewett and Arias reluctantly went to the headquarters, formerly a six-story building that the quake had reduced to a smoking heap. As the two Americans got out of their car, several street kids yelled at them and pointed to the crumbled building next door.

"People are alive in there!" the frantic kids cried out. "We heard them!"

Pointing to the ruins of the naval headquarters, Jewett told Arias, "The hell with this. I'm not risking my neck for some plans when we've got a chance to save some lives."

The two scurried over to the collapsed structure and split up, each entering a separate narrow opening that led into the rubble. Armed with a small flashlight, hunting knife, and digging tool fashioned out of rebar, Jewett picked his way through the smoky, unstable jumble of concrete and twisted steel.

Minutes into his search, the ground began shaking from one of the 1,100 aftershocks that struck the area over a twelve-day period. The crevice he had squirmed into suddenly become narrower as the rubble shifted from the tremor. He realized he had made a big mistake, and unnecessarily put his life in extreme danger. *Damn, no one knows I'm here except Jimmy. If something bad should happen, I'm dead meat.*

Thinking he heard moaning from a survivor, he pressed on. He encountered several small fires, any one of which he knew could flare up. His hand moved to his shirt pocket, where his fingers caressed a .22 magnum High Standard derringer. There only one reason to carry the gun down here. Jewett had no intention of burning to death should one of the fires burst into an inferno. If he had to, if there was no way out, he'd use the pistol on himself. But he quickly put that thought out of his mind. *I'm not going to die in here, at least not today.*

When Jewett reached the basement, his flashlight revealed an underground parking garage filled with cars. Water from broken pipes had seeped in, turning the garage into a death pool where a half a dozen bodies were floating.

Jewett started to feel sick from an unpleasant, odd smell. Then he realized that Mexican soldiers on the surface were fumigating, not knowing or caring if there were people in the rubble. The sight of the bloated bodies and the smell of the fumes from above triggered a severe bout of nausea, so he turned around to head for the surface.

But suddenly he couldn't budge. Something was holding him back. Fear surged through him like electricity and his imagination ran wild. *Oh God! I can't move. One of those corpses has grabbed my leg! He's trying to drag me down into that stinking water!* Jewett knew it was impossible, but he couldn't control those outlandish thoughts.

Just a razor's edge from complete panic, Jewett focused for a second on the derringer in his shirt pocket. *I can always escape with a bullet in my brain*, he told himself. He took a deep breath, then dismissed as insane the thought that a dead man was trying to lug him down into the catacombs of the quake.

"Wait a minute, wait a minute," Jewett told himself out loud. "Remember your training. Make a survey of your surroundings." The words started to calm him. "Take a couple of breaths and try to loosen up."

He realized that the darkness and the stench of decaying flesh combined with fumigation chemicals had momentarily ripped away his grip on reality. Recovering from his mental nightmare, he shined his flashlight over his body and discovered that his belt was caught on a bent piece of steel rebar. So much for the corpse grabbing him. He quickly freed himself and scrambled to the surface without searching further.

Arias was back on top, reporting he hadn't found anyone to save. Jewett had nearly lost his life, taking a wild risk for nothing. He decided there would be no more spur-of-the-moment dives into the rubble. From now on, he would lead only organized rescue operations.

Jewett placated Mexican authorities by telling them he was there to search for trapped Americans. But his real mission was to rescue anyone still alive. Then he called his home base in Miami for reinforcements. Jewett told Joaquim Del Quado, a Miami rescue firefighter, "Grab whatever tools you can. Then get six or seven men together. I don't care who they are, as long as they're firefighters or paramedics and they can speak Spanish. When you have all that, get on a jet and get down here."

Del Quado and his contingent were in the air in less than twenty-four hours.

Jewett's biggest missions centered on two buildings: Hospitale Generale and Hospitale Benito Juarez. The structures, within a mile of each other, had collapsed, trapping hundreds of medical personnel, patients, visitors, and babies.

The rescuers started work at Hospitale Benito Juarez, a twelve-story building that had been reduced to a pancaked tomb for hundreds of people. A Mexican physician pleaded with Jewett to find and rescue thirty-two medical students who were somewhere beneath the rubble. The doctor was frantic. One of the students was his son.

Once inside the debris, Jewett made contact with a man trapped in a crevice on the other side of a wall of crumbled concrete. "I think I'm having a heart attack," the man gasped. "But don't worry about me. Try to rescue the babies. I can hear them nearby."

Jewett and his men worked their way deeper into the wreckage, chopping at concrete obstacles with their chisels and hammers until they opened up a small void no more than three feet high and room enough for one adult to squeeze into. To their joy, they discovered six infants—miraculously, all alive. The babies had fallen five stories from the nursery on the seventh floor to the level that had once been the second floor. Clenching and unclenching their fists, the infants were bruised, weak, and dehydrated, but otherwise in remarkably good shape, considering their hellish first days of life.

The babies were spared because they were in strong stainless steel cribs. When a large chunk of the ceiling collapsed from the earthquake, it landed and rested on top of the cribs. Their steel sides supported the slab, sheltering the infants.

When Jewett slipped into the void, he faced a big problem. He couldn't remove the rubble because it was too heavy. He couldn't cut through the steel slats on the sides of the cribs without the slab falling down and crushing the babies. He had virtually no room to maneuver. The only way to retrieve each infant was to go underneath the crib, cut a hole in the mattress and pull the baby out from the bottom.

However, two cribs presented an added complication. In each case, the body of a dead nurse was wedged underneath, trapped by immovable chunks of concrete. The solution required an incredibly strong stomach and an even stronger will to do what had to be done, no matter how revolting or ghastly it was.

Jewett pulled out his Rambo knife and cut through the bodies of the dead nurses so he could reach the cribs. Then he removed all the infants.

Ruins of Horror

The following day, Jewett's team broke a hole into the chamber that had imprisoned the terrified man who thought he was having a heart attack. Fortunately, he had suffered nothing more than a panic attack, an attack that was alleviated by the sheer happiness of learning his tip led to the rescue of six babies.

The thirty-two trapped medical students weren't so lucky. None made it out alive.

If dealing with constant tremors, shifting rubble, and decaying bodies weren't difficult enough, Jewett's team faced another hazard: the Mexican Army. Over Jewett's objections, the military continued to bulldoze nearby buildings. This caused vibrations that made the work at the hospitals even more dangerous, compelling Jewett to scrap some rescue efforts.

"It would be a good thing if those bulldozers weren't able to work anymore," Jewett said wistfully to his team.

That night, Jimmy Arias and a Mexican teenager whom he'd befriended slipped away from the group. The next day, the soldiers couldn't start the heavy machines. Perplexed, the soldiers discovered parts were broken or missing. It took two days before the bulldozers roared back into action.

At one point, Jewett and his men went to the remains of a nearby building and pleaded for the Army to stop bulldozing so the search for survivors could continue at the hospital. The soldiers responded by pointing rifles at them, forcing them to back away so that bulldozers could level the site.

But the heavy equipment was blocked by anguished Mexican civilians who were holding vigil, hoping rescuers could find trapped relatives or at least retrieve bodies for burial. When the soldiers moved in, the crowd jeered and threw rocks, threatening to riot until the military withdrew and agreed to let Jewett and his people work on the two hospitals.

Amazingly, when they were off duty, some of the Mexican soldiers dumped their rifles and uniforms, put on civilian clothes, and returned to the sites to assist Jewett's teams. Hundreds of Mexican volunteers formed bucket brigades, carefully moving debris. Others joined squads who slowly walked on top of the ruins, listening for any signs of life.

Sometimes two days passed before they heard anything. Then, usually after a severe aftershock that caused a shift in the rubble, voices were heard from half a dozen spots at once, all screaming, crying, and begging for help. Tragically, most died before rescuers could find them.

Almost daily, Jewett encountered conflicting scenes of heartbreak and hope. In a room near the collapsed nursery, he found the lifeless body of a woman clutching a baby girl to her breast. Jewett gently pulled the infant away and discovered to his shock that the baby was still alive although her jaw was broken. Jewett whisked her to safety.

Nearly nine days after the earth first shook, Jewett found another baby who was alive. But the infant's head was compressed because it was lodged between two heavy slabs of concrete. The weight of the slabs had flattened the soft bones of his skull. The baby was in such a delicate position that any further movement of the concrete would likely squash him to death.

"This kid has waited nine days for us to save him, let's not rush this job," Jewett told his colleagues. "If we don't do it right, the slab will crush his head."

To rescue him, Jewett had to dig past the baby to a spot where he could shore up the piece of concrete resting on top of the infant's head. Once Jewett did that, the team then chipped away at the slab below the child. It took seventeen grueling hours but they finally brought him out to safety.

Jewett tried hard to keep his emotions in check—to remain hardened to the gruesome, often heartrending scenes he encountered—because there was no other way he could complete his mission. To let loose emotionally would mean weeping over every body until he was wrung out and useless.

Nevertheless, he came upon one situation that punctured his bulletproof emotional veneer.

It happened at Hospitale Generale, where a foreign rescue crew told him that although they hadn't reached the nursery, they were convinced that none of the babies had survived.

But Jewett wanted to see for himself. His instincts were telling him to search the area again. So he and Mexican physician Julio Chavez snaked their way through the underground jumble and started chopping at the flooring. After a couple of minutes Jewett looked down into a six-inch-wide hole he made and saw a tragic sight that left him deeply moved. One nurse was draped over another nurse so that their lifeless bodies had formed a macabre cross. It appeared as though they were killed by a large piece of rubble that had fallen on them.

What touched a chord with Jewett was the shiny, long, black hair of the nurse on top. He found it strange that her hair looked liked it had been carefully arranged so that it rested inside the bottom drawer of an open metal filing cabinet a foot away from her head. *Why would a woman use her last breath to do something like that?* he wondered.

It was an eerie sight, one that made the veteran of dozens of rescues and major disasters want to leave. As Jewett started to back away from the hole, he was grabbed by Dr. Chavez, who said, "Wait, something is moving down there."

Jewett listened but couldn't hear anything. "Let's go," he said. "There's nothing here but a tomb for a pair of nurses—and it smells really bad." He backed away, but again Dr. Chavez clutched his arm.

"No, don't go," the doctor insisted. "I definitely heard a baby cry." He lowered his stethoscope through the hole. "Listen for yourself." Dr. Chavez offered him the stethoscope.

Jewett listened carefully and perked up. "I can hear movement. You might be right."

Dr. Chavez didn't hear him. At that moment, the physician was overcome by the stench and started throwing up.

Jewett chipped at the hole until he widened it to about two feet across, barely big enough for him to slip through. He dropped down next to the two nurses, but found no signs of life.

Then he stared at the nurse with the long hair. He imagined how beautiful it must have been cascading down past her waist. *I bet when she danced, she wore her hair down so it would swing like the colorful skirts they wear down here. Such beautiful hair. Why did she put it in a cabinet? It seems so crazy.*

Suddenly, he glimpsed a slight movement coming from the bottom drawer. He crawled as close to the cabinet as he could and with an ax in one hand ready to strike at a possible rat inside, he opened the drawer. He didn't see anything at first so he gently began to unfold the silky hair. *It's like she was putting it into storage, like a blanket that's put away for the summer.*

A second later, Jewett gasped in astonishment. Inside the drawer, covered by the nurse's hair, was an infant boy. And he was alive. "Doc, you were right!" Jewett yelled.

It looked like the baby had been born just hours before the earthquake struck. The infant had been placed in the drawer and delicately wrapped in the nurse's long hair. The hair acted as a blanket to keep the baby warm and as a filter to shield him from the dust. On the infant's feet were a pair of hospital slippers, too big for his tiny feet but placed so that they acted like leggings to ward off the night chill.

Jewett gently freed the baby from the nurse's hair and eased him out of the cabinet drawer that had protected him for all six days of his life.

No one would ever know exactly what happened in those last desperate moments for the nurse, but Jewett would never stop thinking about the heroic act of this selfless woman, one of thousands of good people who were forever lost in the disaster.

The toll would have been higher if it hadn't been for Jewett and his team. After their twelve-day stint of exhaustive, painstaking, dangerous work in the rubble of the two hospitals, they had rescued a total of forty-two babies and seventy-seven adults.

CINDIA'S HERO

Lieutenant Joseph Clerici and the men of Ladder 11 in Manhattan were heading back to the station after rescuing a couple of people stranded in a stuck elevator when the call came in over the radio: "Fire in an apartment building, Avenue C and 9th Street." It was just before midnight, May 14, 1995.

Because Clerici and his crew were two blocks away, they arrived first. The fire was in a five-story walk-up, and the top two floors were engulfed in white-hot flames and billowing smoke. Most of the panic-stricken people who had lived in the building had already streamed out into the night.

"There're people inside!" one woman screamed at Clerici, a thirty-nine-year-old veteran fireman.

Even though the other fire engines had not arrived, which meant there were no hoses to fight the blaze, Clerici and two other firefighters dashed into the building and searched its smoke-filled corridors from the first floor through the third and found no one.

When they reached the fourth floor, they spotted a petite, dark-haired woman in a silky pink nightgown wailing hysterically, "Cindia! Cindia!" She was banging on a locked apartment door with a hammer, ramming it with her shoulder and using every ounce of strength she could muster in a frantic attempt to batter it down. Her toes were bleeding, leaving splotches of blood on the door where she had been kicking it.

"Cindia! Cindia!" she shrieked, as she bashed on the door with the hammer, then with her arms and fists. In one hand, Clerici noticed, she clutched a doorknob. Turning to the firefighters, she cried, "She's inside! My daughter, my daughter! Please help me!"

Just hours earlier, the woman, Angela Rojas, had tucked her six-year-old daughter Cindia into bed. The child was wearing a pink-and-white silk nightgown that matched her mother's. Both nightgowns had been Mother's Day gifts from Angela's husband, Leo.

After Angela had put their daughter to bed, Leo lit a prayer candle for his mother in the living room. He then went to the restaurant where he worked as a sous chef and Angela dozed off on the couch. A couple of hours later, firefighters would later conclude, one of the family's two pet cats overturned the candle, igniting the fire.

Angela was jolted awake by the smell of smoke. She saw flames in the living room and then dashed into the apartment building's hallway to call for help. As soon as she opened the apartment door and stepped into the hall, a back draft from the flames slammed it shut. When she tried to open it again, she discovered to her horror that the door was locked. In her frenzy to open it, she yanked the knob off in her hand. Inside, she heard Cindia crying out, "Mommy! Mommy!"

A neighbor brought out a hammer, and Angela attacked the door with fury as Cindia's voice grew fainter and the smoke grew thicker. Soon Cindia stopped calling for her mommy. The only sounds inside were the crackling of the flames.

By the time Clerici reached the anguished woman, she was spent, her face streaked with soot and tears, her hands and toes red and bloody from hitting the door. "Please, please!" she sobbed, falling to her knees. "My daughter is inside! Save her!"

"Oh my God," Clerici murmured, noticing smoke coming out from under the door. "How old is she?"

"Six. Cindia is only six. She's in the back bedroom."

The firefighters pushed Angela aside and rammed against the door. It didn't budge. Finally, they pried the door open with special tools and were hit in the face with black smoke so dense that it shot out into the hall in the shape of the doorway. *My God, it's coming out square,* Clerici said to himself.

"Cindia! Cindia!" Angela screamed.

Clerici paused to make a quick assessment of the burning apartment. *No one can possibly be alive in there,* he thought. *If the flames didn't kill her, the smoke probably did.*

Then an image flashed in his mind. It was that of a little blond girl with dazzling blue eyes and a pixie smile. It was his daughter Katherine, who was the same age as Cindia. Clerici's heart sank at the thought of his own little girl trapped by flames and smoke. He knew instantly that he must try to save Cindia.

"I'm going in," he told the other firefighters.

The apartment was a railroad flat, so to reach Cindia's room, he would have to grope in the darkness and the deadly flames through two other large rooms. Because the smoke had not sunk all the way to the floor, there was about a foot and a half layer of breathable air. It was just enough for a man to crawl through, just enough if he kept his face pressed to the floor.

"I've only got a small window of opportunity," he said, knowing how fires can turn deadly in a matter of seconds. "I've got to go right now."

Cindia's Hero

Clerici dropped to the floor and crawled on his belly into the fiery hell. He tried to move forward, but couldn't get his bearings. So he put his left hand on the wall and used his right to drag his body forward. A nerve-racking minute went by as he pulled himself through one room, then the next, every so often dodging a burning cinder that had fallen in his path.

Outside the apartment behind him, he heard the muffled cries of Angela still screeching, "Cindia! Cindia!" He also heard sirens, and knew that more help was arriving. It would eventually take fourteen trucks and sixty-two firefighters to put out the blaze.

But Clerici had only one thing on his mind: saving Cindia.

Taking short, quick breaths of air under the sinking smoke, he finally made it to the door of the child's bedroom. He prayed that she had stayed on or near the bed, otherwise his chances of finding her would be next to zero. Blind from the smoke, he felt around until he touched the bed. He reached up and brought his palm down onto the flat surface, but jerked it back quickly. The mattress was on fire. Everything in the room was glowing red.

He tried again, but his fingers touched nothing that felt like a body. *Cindia isn't on the burning bed, so where is she?* Clerici wondered. *I hope she didn't hide in the closet.* He'd seen another child do that years earlier with fatal results. *Maybe she ran into another room, or tried to climb out the window. Damn, I can't see a thing.*

By now the deadly, choking smoke had settled lower to the floor. Clerici was gasping for air, his face pressed against the cracks in the floorboards.

"Joe! Get out of there!" shouted one of the firefighters.

"I need more time!" he yelled back.

Not sure where to go or what to do next, Clerici started frantically running his hands on the floor around the bed, until he hit something spongy and hot. It was a leg. He had found Cindia. She was under the bed curled up in the fetal position, clutching her two pet cats, both dead. She wasn't moving. And her nightgown was on fire.

Clerici pulled her little body against his fireproof coat and snuffed out the flames on her nightgown. But he couldn't feel her breathing or detect any sign of life. He could tell that she was severely burned from the way her skin felt—it was peeling off in his hand. She was probably past help, he knew, but he couldn't give up.

"I got her!" he yelled to the other firefighters still at the door. "But I can't see how to get out of here!"

With Cindia's body under his, Clerici blindly slid out of the girl's smoky black room, guided by the voices of his fellow firefighters from Ladder 11. "This way, Joe! Come on!" they called out. He dragged himself and the inert, smoldering little girl through the master bedroom, then the living room.

Every second, the smoke was sinking closer to the floor, reducing the small layer of air that was keeping him alive. *Like the picture going off on one of those old TVs,* Clerici thought. His progress was slow, too slow. *I think I'm going to die here.*

"Get the hell out of there!" one of the firefighters shouted.

Clerici knew that he could move faster on his own without the girl. *She's probably dead anyway,* he told himself. *Am I going to die here with this dead kid? If I leave her, I might have a chance.* For a brief moment, he thought about dropping her and saving himself. But he just couldn't do it. There was something about a child that always made him, and every firefighter he knew, go the extra length.

Maybe this kid's still alive. I can't leave her. So he pressed on. By now the smoke had reached the floor.

Clerici held his breath and pounded on the floor so his partners could find him. Seconds later, they yanked Clerici and the girl out of the apartment and into the hallway.

Angela, clutching the arm of a priest, screamed for joy. But when she saw her lifeless, burned child, she threw her body over Cindia. "My baby! My baby!" she sobbed.

While one paramedic rushed to the gagging, coughing Clerici to give him oxygen, another tried to revive the little girl with oxygen and CPR. "I don't have a pulse," said the paramedic who quickly inserted a tube down her throat. As the paramedics whisked her past Clerici toward a waiting ambulance, he murmured, "C'mon, honey, you can make it. You've got to make it." Once again, the image of his beloved daughter Katherine flashed in his mind. He could only imagine the horror and anguish that Angela was suffering at that moment.

When Clerici's breathing and strength returned after taking the oxygen, he perked up even more when word came back to him that the paramedics had revived Cindia on the way to the hospital. "Thank God," he said. "She wasn't dead after all."

Although he took comfort in hearing that Cindia was alive, he knew the odds were stacked against her. In his fifteen years on the job, he'd seen many fire victims who pulled through despite hideous burns. But through his long career, he knew of no child with burns as bad as Cindia's who had survived more than a week.

When the exhausted firefighter got home in the early hours of May 15, he tiptoed into the bedroom of his sleeping daughter and hugged her tightly. He couldn't let go of her. But he also couldn't let go of the mental picture he had of the burned Cindia.

Cindia's Hero

For days, he was afraid to make a phone call to the hospital, afraid to hear a doctor tell him that Cindia had died. He finally worked up the courage to find out her status. To his surprise, he learned she was still alive, but barely clinging to life. Cindia suffered third-degree burns over 50 percent of her body, and her lungs had been so badly damaged by smoke that she could not breathe on her own. The fingers on her right hand had been burned off, and other burns had gone through to the bone. She was kept in a drug-induced coma for a month because the pain from her burns was unbearable. Her doctors had done so many skin grafts on her that they soon lost track of the number.

Clerici kept calling the hospital regularly to check on her progress. No one in Cindia's family knew he was calling or even knew the name of the firefighter who had rescued their little girl.

Once Cindia came out of her coma, Clerici stopped calling. He figured that his job was done, he had saved her life, and now he didn't want to intrude upon it.

In time, the plucky girl beat the odds, and weeks later she walked out of the hospital to begin a new life. It would be a hard struggle to make her place in the world, especially with burns that disfigured her face. Thoughtless people stared at her and mean children called her names, but Cindia stayed strong and tried to play like other kids her age. She even learned to ride a bike despite her injuries.

One day a newspaper photographer saw her, took her picture, and arranged for a reporter to write about her life. With help from the reporter, Leo and Angela Rojas tracked down Clerici and invited him to their home.

Days later, a man in the dark blue uniform of a fire captain—Clerici had been promoted—came to visit the family's new apartment. He carried a huge basket filled with teddy bears because he had learned she collected them. Cindia, in a pretty velvet dress, was shy at first.

"Hi," Clerici said. "My name is Joe." As he unwrapped the basket, he said, "I have a little girl the same age as you. She helped me pick these out for you." He handed her a big teddy bear. Cindia clutched it close to her chest and beamed.

Later, after Clerici left, Cindia told her mother, "I know what I'm going to name my new teddy bear."

"What name did you pick?" asked Angela.

"Joe, of course."

A WEIGHTY DILEMMA

Boston firefighter Bill Shea jumped off the back of the rescue truck as it pulled up in front of the eleven-story Paramount Hotel in the city's "Combat Zone," an area of strip clubs, bars, and cheap hotels.

His mind struggled to register what his eyes were seeing—flames were spewing out of a gaping chasm directly in front of the hotel. A moat of fire where a fifteen-foot-wide sidewalk once stood now stretched across the width of the building. On the other side of the flames, at the entrance to a smoke-filled lobby, a soot-covered man in tattered clothes staggered to his feet. Above him, a lifeless, fire-blackened body was draped over a second floor balcony rail.

"Holy cow, what the hell is this?" Shea shouted to his two partners.

For Shea, the night would turn into a strange

life-and-death struggle that rattled his brain with an incongruous mix of calamity and hilarity.

The call had come in by telephone and alarm box on the frigid, windy night of January 28, 1966. Although there had been no word of exactly what firemen were about to face, they figured they would have a tough fight on their hands because gusts were blowing over 40 mph and temperatures had dipped into the low teens.

Shea and his two fellow firemen were the first to arrive at the scene of destruction. They parked several yards away from the fiery hole because the street in front of the seedy hotel had been blown to bits, its flying chunks of concrete crushing nearby parked cars.

"That must have been one hell of an explosion," one of the firefighters said.

"Looks like gas," Shea said. "Nothing else could do this kind of damage."

The firemen stared at the burning moat, trying to figure out what to do next. Just then Shea peered through the smoke and leaping flames and spotted a man wobbling in the hotel's doorway. His face was streaked with sweat, blood, and soot; his clothes were in shreds.

"Help me, please!" the man pleaded. "Please, I'm burned!" Then the man turned and slowly lifted his arm and pointed into the smoky darkness of the

A Weighty Dilemma

hotel lobby. "People in here are hurt bad. They need help. They're dying."

That's all Shea needed to hear. "Let's move!" he shouted to his partners.

To help survivors of the blast, the firefighters needed to cross the fifteen-foot-wide moat of fire. But how? Short of flying, there seemed to be no quick way to do it. Then Shea had an idea. "Let's get a ladder. We'll build a bridge."

The two other firefighters grabbed a ladder from their truck and brought it to him. The ladder was long enough to span the fiery hole to the front door, but it wouldn't protect them from the flames underneath them. Shea hastily glanced around for something, anything, he could use as a shield. Then he found it—an enormous metal sign, an advertisement for Coca-Cola, that lay nearby. It had adorned the building until it was blown off in the blast. *This'll keep our toes from getting burned,* he thought as he seized the big piece of tin and lugged it over to his partners.

They set the ladder so it lay across the flaming moat and then placed the metal sign over the ladder, hoping it would become a bridge of rescue for the people trapped and dying in the burning hotel.

The firefighters had to move fast before the tin sign turned from a shield into a frying pan. But they could go only one at a time.

Ignoring the flames licking up on either side of the Coke sign, Shea scampered across the fiery gap and was quickly followed by the other two.

"There's a lot of work for everybody tonight," Shea said as the other fire companies started rolling in and unraveling their hoses. He was grateful that he wasn't on a hose truck because that meant he would have to stay outside and direct a stream of water in the bitter cold. Winter had sunk its teeth deep into Boston. Hoses would freeze and the spray from their streams would eventually turn everything to ice. It would be pretty, but potentially deadly. Just walking would be a challenge.

Once on the other side of the fiery hole, Shea caught a glimpse of the death toll the blast had caused. Bodies of guests were strewn at odd angles. "I hope there isn't going to be another explosion," Shea told his partners. "This fire is bad enough."

When he reached the dazed and burned man at the doorway, Shea handed him off to his partners. "Get him to an ambulance," he ordered. They hustled the injured man onto the ladder, guiding him safely across. The way they gingerly but swiftly moved over the flames reminded Shea of people walking on beds of red-hot coals.

Shea then turned and moved cautiously inside the hotel alone. Fortunately, the smoke wasn't too bad. He could see a couple of feet in front of him as

A Weighty Dilemma

he picked his way over the debris-strewn floor of what had once been the lobby.

About thirty feet inside, he stopped dead in his tracks. *My God, there's no floor anymore,* Shea said to himself. He now stood at the edge of a gaping hole and looked down into the building's basement, about fourteen feet below.

Smoke curled up from a dozen small blazes that looked like campfires of the damned in a dark, smelly world of blackened rubble. *Like a place where the devil would live,* he thought. Suddenly, to his horror, he noticed that among the rubble were the remains of burn victims. *God, that's not debris. Those are human arms and legs down there. I wonder if anyone is alive.*

Almost immediately he got his answer. "Help me! Help me! Don't let me die!" shrieked a woman in the darkness. Shea stared down in the direction of the panicky voice and saw a large woman stumbling over the debris directly below him. She looked up at him with her arms outstretched, imploring him to save her.

"Oh God, she's one of those plus-sizes," he groaned under his breath. He figured she weighed at least 250 pounds. She was wailing as the flames inched their way toward her. He knew if he didn't do something now, she would be burned alive.

Just what I wanted—a fat woman, he said to

himself sarcastically. *Why oh why don't I ever get one of those 110-pound blond cuties I see in all the movies?*

The brawny thirty-one-year-old firefighter, who stood five foot ten and weighed 175 pounds, pondered how he was going to rescue her. As the situation became more intense, his thoughts and emotions swirled around as crazily as the smoke in the hole. *How can I get her out of there? A small crane might do the trick.* Then he started to get angry. *Why did she have to put me in this predicament?* He worked himself into a fury. He couldn't remember ever being more ticked off at a stranger in his whole life. *I'm going to have to risk my life to save this fat, shrieking woman who I don't even know.*

The woman's plaintive cries pierced the smoky hole. The advancing flames were bright enough for him to see the tears streaking down her face.

I can't leave her, he thought. *This is my job. Okay, so how am I going to get down to her? And even more to the point, with her weight, how am I going to get her out?* Hearing her scream again, he told himself, *That's enough thinking. There's only one thing to do, so do it!*

With that, he jumped down into the flame-filled basement and immediately felt the heat of the fire starting to sting his face. Scattered around the room were crushed bodies, some covered by chunks of concrete and others burning in the flames.

There's nothing I can do for them now, he thought. *I've got more than enough to handle with this hunk of woman.*

The small blazes were growing larger and joining up with one another. Within a matter of minutes, the basement was going to be one big flame pit.

Whatever I do, I'd better do it fast, he told himself.

He could see that the woman was not going to be much help. Aside from her size, she was in a big panic. "Get me out, get me out! We're going to burn! I don't want to die!" she screamed over and over.

"Stay calm. I'll get you out of here. Everything's going to be okay," he replied, giving her the standard fireman's line. But Shea wasn't sure that he could pull off this rescue, not with her weight.

It didn't really matter what he said to comfort her because the woman just kept shrieking, "Save me! Save me!" She was in such a frenzy that she ignored his repeated reassurances.

Save her? he thought. *If these flames get much closer to us, she may find herself all alone. I'll try to climb back up and save myself. It will be an interesting test to see if I stay with her.*

Shea was usually not a nervous man and had enjoyed every minute of his work in the fire department since joining a decade earlier. He had taken some chances in his life, and even put himself in terrible danger to rescue others. This time, he thought, jumping into the flames might not have been such a good idea. *How the hell are we going to get out of here?*

By now his face and hands were singed by the flames, causing the same kind of pain as a severe sunburn. The fire was closing in on them from all sides. *We've got maybe two minutes, probably less,* he figured.

"We can't stay here any longer, so we better move," Shea told her. "But where?" He hurriedly looked to his left and right, to the front and to the back, searching for a way to escape from the menacing ring of fire.

Through the flames and smoke he saw a five-foot-tall pile of concrete rubble about thirty feet away. It didn't look high enough to get them out, but at least it would buy them some time before the fire reached them.

If I can get her up on that pile, maybe I can figure a way to get her out, he thought.

Grabbing her by the hand, he shouted, "Let's go!" She screamed in response.

Refusing to let go of her, he yanked her toward a spot in the ring of fire where the flames were at their lowest and jumped over them. Then, with the braying woman in tow, he weaved his way past patches of fire, broken pipes, and splintered wood to the concrete heap.

All this woman can do is scream and cry, he thought. Once again, anger reared up inside him. *Why her? Why me? Why am I dragging her along? She can't even move on her own. She's helpless and isn't doing anything to help either one of us.*

The wave of anger quickly passed, and the instincts of the veteran fireman kicked in. *It doesn't matter. I have to find a way to save her, and me.* For the first time he was beginning to think he could die in there. He knew he had to keep a level head if they were to survive. This was no time to be consumed by rage or blame the shrieking woman for landing him in a fire-filled basement.

When they reached the heap of rubble, he climbed up a few feet, turned around, grasped her fleshy arms and pulled her up toward him. Then he repeated it until they had reached the top.

Shea looked up at the jagged opening to the floor above him. From the top of the pile, he could see they were nearly ten feet shy of the lobby floor. The fire had reached the bottom of the heap and was beginning to snake its way up toward them.

Now what do I do? he wondered. *Think fast, think fast.*

Looking into her fright-filled eyes, he placed his hands on her beefy arms and said, "Okay, listen to me carefully. I'm going to help you climb on my shoulders and then you'll be able to reach the floor up there. It's our only hope."

The woman cried, "Oh, no!"

"Oh, yes," he snapped back. "We can do this."

Shea was a solidly built man and in good shape, but nevertheless, this woman outweighed him by at least seventy-five pounds. Even if he was able to hoist her up, there was no guarantee that she had the strength to pull herself out onto the lobby floor. And then there was the question of how he was going to get out. But he didn't have time to think about that. He could feel the flames licking at the back of his turnout coat.

With her back to him, Shea squatted down as low as he could go and then had her step back. He placed both hands on her buttocks in an effort to help lift her over his head so she could straddle his shoulders. *I've got more ass in my hands than any man could possibly need*, he joked to himself.

Once she finally was able to wrap her legs around the back of his head, Shea wisecracked, "I guess we'll have to get engaged after this."

The woman kept blubbering.

Now comes the really hard part, Shea thought. Straining against the heavy weight on his shoulders, the fireman grunted and groaned and shakily straightened up.

A Weighty Dilemma

His thighs quivering and torso shaking, he ordered, "Okay, now stand up on my shoulders and try to grab the edge of the floor." She placed her feet on his shoulders and he clutched her ankles. He was straining so much he could barely get the words out. "Hurry and grab the top. I can't hold you much longer."

He felt her sweaty, slippery ankles slip through his hands, and she tumbled back onto the pile of debris, almost sending him rolling into the flames, which were now enclosing them in a circle of death that was shrinking by the second.

"Okay, we'll try it again," Shea told her firmly. She responded with a whimper.

He bent over, grabbed her on the underside of her buttocks and helped her get on his shoulders. "Yeah, we're definitely engaged now," he said. "I suppose I'm going to have to marry you no matter what."

But like before, the woman tumbled off him, leaving her sobbing on the pile. Flames were now reaching his boots and scorching the back of his turnout coat.

Whatever sense of humor Shea possessed was now long gone, replaced with a sense of doom. *We have only seconds left. I don't know if I'm going to get out of here alive. I don't know if I'm going to be strong enough to do this. But it's our only chance.*

"Come on," he urged her. "One more try."

The woman wailed louder but did what she was told. As she climbed onto his shoulders, he thought, *If I lose her again, I may just run. Hey, quit thinking like that. I could never do that, not if I ever want to look myself in the mirror again. She is in mortal danger. I have to try to get her out.* He crouched down, trying once again to grab the hysterical woman. He wondered how long it would be before the flames flirting with his heavy coat would burn through to his flesh.

As the sobbing woman tried to stand up on his shoulders, Shea began to wobble. He simply wasn't strong enough to handle her weight. "Where the hell are my pals?" he muttered.

"Shea, is that you?"

Shea looked up and breathed an enormous sigh of relief. Gazing down from the hole in the lobby floor were his two partners who, after helping the burned man in the doorway to an ambulance, had returned to find Shea.

"What the hell took you so long?" Shea grumbled.

Emboldened with the faith that he and the crying woman were about to be saved, Shea found renewed strength and steadied himself long enough for each of the firefighters above to reach down and grab an arm of the still wailing woman and pull her out.

"Don't spend too much time getting to know her," Shea yelled up. "It's getting a little warm down here."

One of the firemen leaned down headfirst into

the hole while his partner held onto his legs. The first firefighter stretched as far as he could until he and Shea could clasp each other's wrists. Then the second fireman at the end of the human chain pulled them up and out of the hole. As Shea flopped onto the lobby floor, he looked down and saw flames consume the pile of debris upon which he had stood seconds earlier.

"I think it's a good time to check out of this joint," he said. His partners escorted him and the blubbering woman out of the lobby and safely across the improvised Coke sign bridge. Seconds after Shea and the woman were placed in separate ambulances, the whole building erupted in flames.

Watching the ambulance carry off the woman, Shea turned to a medic and deadpanned, "She didn't even say good-bye, and we had gotten very intimate down there in the basement."

Shea, who like the woman suffered burns to his face and hands, was taken to Massachusetts General Hospital where he was rolled into the hectic emergency room. A doctor gave Shea a cursory examination and shoved him and his gurney into a corner.

In the controlled chaos of the ER, scurrying nurses and doctors ignored him and tended to more serious casualties from the blaze. Victims, many of them badly burned or bleeding, were crying and moaning.

As Shea watched the ER team in action, a "fire rep"—a firefighter assigned to hospital duty to look out for the interests of other members of the department—showed up. "Are you here to hold my hand?" Shea asked him.

A half hour later Shea told him, "I've had enough rest now. Get me out of here."

"Where do you want to go?" asked the rep.

"Back to the fire."

So Shea jumped off his gurney and walked out with the rep to a fire department car and headed back to the Paramount, where the firefighters had finally knocked down the blaze.

"Hey, anybody know where the Rescue Company is?" Shea yelled to a group of firemen.

"In the basement," came the response.

"That's good. I know how to get there."

He rejoined his partners and spent the rest of the night retrieving the dead. By morning ten bodies had been recovered from the ruins. Another victim lingered for a few days before dying. More than fifty people were injured.

Fire investigators concluded that a gas leak in the basement had sparked the explosion, which sent the second-floor cocktail lounge plunging through the lobby and into the basement. The lady Shea rescued was the only one from the lounge to survive the fall.

A Weighty Dilemma

Shea received his department's top award, the John Fitzgerald Medal of Valor, for his bravery in saving the woman's life. He never saw her again or exchanged any messages with her. In fact, she never thanked him. But that didn't bother Shea. He did his job and did it well. And, more importantly, she was alive.

"You know, she never tried to get in touch with me after our little interlude in the basement," Shea said after receiving the medal. "I thought we had really started something down there."

RESCUE ON THE RUNWAY

Precious seconds were ticking away for airport fireman Dave Russell. Swirling flames were pawing at him the moment he reached the burning cracked-up fighter jet. If Russell didn't act fast, the injured pilot in the cockpit would die a horrible death.

For that matter, Russell would likely perish too. The flames had reached the plane's Gatling gun and its magazine of 20-millimeter shells. At any moment now, the ammunition could explode, spraying rogue shells in all directions. As if that wasn't hazardous enough, the fire had reached an auxiliary power unit that, if burned, would release poisonous gas. Then, of course, he faced the danger of fuel mixing with the flames.

Shoving those concerns out of his mind, Russell reached the smoke-filled cockpit where he encountered another hazard: The flames could trigger the explosives used in the jettison system of the rocket-propelled ejection seat.

Seconds, just seconds, were all the time Russell had left to open the canopy and rescue the pilot before they both faced certain death by flames, bullets, explosives, or gas.

"Damn it!" yelled Russell. "It's jammed!"

Now was the time Russell needed to muster his strength and maintain his wits—traits that had always served him well over the years. After all, the attributes of a good fireman were in his genes. As a fourth-generation firefighter, he had smoke coursing through his veins from the day he was born.

The family's firefighting tradition began with Russell's great-grandfather, a blacksmith who shoed all the horses for the Fairfield, Connecticut, Fire Department. His grandfather was a fireman there. Then his father joined the department as a firefighter and climbed the ranks to become fire chief.

So it seemed only natural that David W. Russell III would be a fireman too. Only, he took a different route, starting his firefighting career in the Air Force, where he remained an airport fireman for eight years. In 1984, he left the service to join the New York City Fire Department, fulfilling a lifelong ambition. He also enlisted in the New York Air National Guard where he was promoted to staff sergeant.

Rescue on the Runway

In the summer of 1992, the thirty-seven-year-old guardsman had gone to Homestead Air Force Base near Miami to take part in war games. He soon found himself waging a battle in a real war of life and death.

It happened on the last day of his two-week duty there. He had been a little bored because the deployment of the war games had been uneventful, but he also had been a little relieved for the same reason.

Russell was sitting with two fellow firefighters on a flight line fire truck in a hangar, trying to stay cool in the sweltering south Florida heat. It was 11:30 A.M., and he was counting the minutes until noon, when he was scheduled to be relieved. He planned to return to his quarters so he could pack for his flight back to New York City and join his wife for the closing on the purchase of their new house in the suburb of Pound Ridge.

Suddenly a voice over the intercom blared: "In-flight emergency! In-flight emergency! An F-16 with control problems . . . five minutes out!"

The call didn't seem to faze Russell. "Probably just the usual," he said to his partners. "We'll drive out and chase this guy down the runway and when he stops rolling, he'll give us a thumbs-up and taxi over to maintenance. No big deal. We used to get these kind of routine calls ten times a day in Germany," he added, referring to his three years of active duty in Bitburg.

However, this emergency would be anything but routine.

The pilot had taken the single-seat, Flying Falcon jet on a test flight after it had undergone extensive maintenance. During a high-speed maneuver, his jet flamed out and stalled, and he lost use of most of his controls. He could have ejected. But with base housing on one side of the field and a civilian residential area on the other, the pilot didn't want to abandon the plane and risk having it crash into a home. However, without the proper controls, the best he could hope for was a crash landing at the airport.

As the firefighters started up the engine to their big crash truck, they glanced skyward and saw the crippled F-16 yawing and pitching during a faster than normal descent. The plane came in hard and slammed into the runway, blowing out the tires and crushing the landing gear. Careening out of control, the jet burst into flames as it skidded and spun across the tarmac and came to rest ablaze on the grassy infield.

"Oh God!" Russell shouted.

Jet fuel was spewing from a broken line just aft of the cockpit where the F-16 had split in two. An eighteen-inch gap in the aluminum skin made it all too easy to see the fuel pouring on the fire.

Russell and his two partners hurriedly donned their "silvers," the silvery fire- and heat-resistant suits designed to protect them from burning jet fuel. They hopped on their fire truck and sped to the wreck, where Russell fired a shot of fire-retardant foam at the flames from a turret-mounted hose.

By now, he expected to see the pilot open the canopy and jump out. But the pilot remained in the smoke-filled cockpit, flailing his arms. Through the smoke, Russell saw flickers of flames grazing the pilot's flight suit.

He's burning and he's disoriented, Russell thought. *He must be badly hurt if he can't get out on his own. I've got to get him out of there.*

Russell reached up into a cabinet in the truck to grab his breathing mask but the mask wouldn't come free from its bracket no matter how hard he yanked. He needed the mask to protect his face from the fire, toxic fumes, and the super-heated air that could damage his lungs.

I can't hang around here any longer yanking at this thing, Russell told himself. *That pilot has zero time left.* So the firefighter made a bold decision. He would go into the flames with his hooded suit but without any face protection or breathing apparatus.

"Your mask!" hollered a fellow guardsman.

"I can't wait. This guy is in real trouble," Russell replied. "He can't get out on his own."

As he ran toward the plane, Russell looked over his shoulder and saw that both his partners didn't have their masks on either. They were in too much of a hurry. The pilot needed to be rescued within the next minute if he had a chance at survival.

Russell, who had two other runway rescues under his belt, went on automatic. Years of constant training with the F-16 had taught him the first thing he needed to do in this situation was get to the emergency control panel located on the left side of the fuselage near the cockpit. Inside the hatch were the controls that would unlatch the canopy, disengage the weapons systems and power sources, and deactivate the rocket-powered Zero-Zero ejection seat that could propel the pilot out of his cockpit even when the plane is on the ground and not moving. Russell knew where all the controls were even with his eyes closed.

Damn, most of the fire is on the left side. That figures, he told himself as he ran toward the plane. Jutting out on the left side near the nose was the menacing cannon of the fully-loaded Gatling gun. It was slightly above the flames and only a few feet away from the emergency control panel. *Whoever designed the F-16 didn't like firefighters very much.*

When Russell reached the panel door, the flames were spreading around the craft and in the cockpit. The pilot looked like he was losing consciousness because his hands weren't flying around the cockpit like they had a minute earlier.

Rescue on the Runway

I've got to move fast before this guy starts inhaling smoke, Russell thought. *I've got to get him out of the ejection seat first before the fire sets it off.* The fire-fighter knew that wasn't supposed to happen, but in a crash all the rules changed. In a crash, he always believed, the number one rule is, "There are no rules."

Okay, all I have to do is open the hatch, pop the canopy, and we'll get him out. Russell gave a tug with his wrench and then another tug, but the door to the emergency control panel wouldn't budge. *Damn! It's jammed!*

He took a quick, nervous glance as the flames reached to the Gatling gun. Russell knew that if the magazine exploded, the 20-millimeter shells could shoot in all directions, killing him, the pilot, other firefighters and even Air Force personnel hundreds of yards away who were watching the scene unfold. *Thank goodness the plane isn't carrying any bombs or rockets—at least none that I can see.*

As if the situation wasn't bad enough, he could hear a machine gun-like rat-tat-tat-a-tat. The sound meant that the fighter plane's emergency propulsion unit, EPU, had been activated. The EPU, an auxiliary power unit that comes on if the jet's engine fails, operated basic hydraulic and electrical systems to keep the plane in the air. It worked on hydrazine, a deadly toxin that can quickly rot a man's liver if inhaled. Air Force fire crews were always warned that if they heard the EPU had been activated and they smelled ammonia—a byproduct of the hydrazine—they needed to leave the area immediately or risk death themselves.

Amid the acrid smell of jet fuel and burning metal and rubber, Russell began getting a whiff of ammonia. *Damn, I wish I had my mask and breather.*

By now firefighters in other trucks began spraying foam on the flames. But that did little good for the trapped pilot who by now had lost consciousness in the fiery, smoky cockpit.

Turning to one of his partners, Russell shouted, "Help me get this hatch open! It's stuck!" Together, grunting and groaning, they finally unlatched the door. "Yes!"

Without barely looking, Russell reached in and pulled the lever that popped the canopy. Then he pulled the safety switches that shut down the weapon systems, deactivated the ejection seat, and turned off the EPU.

He and his two partners reached into the flaming cockpit and pulled out the limp body of the airman, whose scorched flight suit was on fire. The firemen snuffed out the flames on his suit and hurriedly handed him off to the paramedics, who rushed him to a waiting ambulance. (The pilot was hospitalized for serious burns over much of his body, but he survived.)

Rescue on the Runway

The distinctive smell of ammonia stinging his nostrils, Russell jumped away from the aircraft and joined one of the hose crews working at the edge of the flames. For several tense minutes, they kept the flow of foam going until the blaze died down and the dangers had passed.

While the smashed jet was still smoldering, Russell and his two partners were ordered to report to the base hospital to undergo blood and lung tests for exposure to hydrazine. The men were lucky. The test results revealed that the firemen hadn't inhaled enough of the poison to do much damage.

After a couple of hours, the trio headed back to their barracks. "My wife isn't going to like this one bit," Russell said to his buddies. "I'm still here and now she's closing on our new house all by herself. She's going to give me zero sympathy."

His mood changed when he arrived at the enlisted quarters. Two cases of cold beer were waiting for the firefighters, compliments of the fighter squadron whose pilot they had helped save. Later, having missed his flight home, Russell let the fighter crews take him to the NCO club, where his money and his partners' money were considered "no good."

"It feels like I won the Super Bowl," said Russell as he was offered another free drink by a grateful F-16 crew chief. "It feels good to help someone."

Russell, who would later receive the New York Air National Guard's Meritorious Service Medal, added, "I know this sounds trite, but I was just doing my job, a job I really love."

THE SEA WITCH DISASTER

The crewmen of the fireboat *Firefighter* stared grimly at the horrific scene in the distance off their bow. A tanker and a freighter that had collided minutes earlier were engulfed in a blaze that was shooting pillars of flames over two hundred feet high—high enough to reach the underbelly of New York's majestic Verrazano-Narrows Bridge. Thick oil oozing from the ruptured hold of the tanker was spreading a ring of fire around the two vessels.

What the *Firefighter* crew couldn't see from that distance were the anxious sailors on the stricken, burning ships huddled in the stern, wondering if they would be rescued before flames reached them. A few sailors, crazed with fear and panic, could no longer stand the excruciating wait, so in desperation they jumped overboard, right into the burning oil and to their deaths.

The Greatest Firefighter Stories Never Told

Now *Firefighter*, the New York Fire Department's biggest fireboat, was racing at its full twelve knots an hour in a daring attempt to rescue the survivors and battle the blaze in a mission fraught with uncommon danger, because it meant conducting the operation in a literal sea of flames.

Around midnight June 2, 1973, the six-hundred-foot-long, 17,902-ton freighter *Sea Witch,* laden with more than seven hundred large metal containers, cast off from a New Jersey warehouse dock. On an outgoing tide, the ship slowly made her way through the vessel-crowded Kill Van Kull, a waterway between Staten Island and New Jersey lined with oil and chemical plants.

At the helm, Captain William Patterson was navigating her into New York Harbor at a brisk seventeen knots an hour when the worst breakdown imaginable happened to the ship—she lost her steering. Captain Patterson and his crew immediately went to auxiliary steering, but that failed too. Suddenly the *Sea Witch* was drifting at the mercy of the notoriously treacherous tides of the narrow entrance to the harbor.

Repeatedly blowing a distress signal, the captain worked furiously in a frenzied attempt to keep the ship in the channel and away from a half dozen loaded oil tankers anchored out in the Narrows between Staten Island and Brooklyn. (As a precaution, it was standard procedure that all tankers remained in the remote

The *Sea Witch* Disaster

anchorage and far from the main part of the city until it was time to sail or unload.)

All control of the *Sea Witch* was lost. Adding to the danger, the ship was loaded to the rails with "red-listed" cargo—freight that could burn or explode. Where it would drift and what it would hit, no one knew.

The six moored tankers were sitting ducks. There was no way they could weigh anchor in time and move out of the path of the crippled vessel. Their fate rested in blind luck.

Miraculously, the *Sea Witch* safely slipped past five of the tankers. But just when it looked as if the ship would drift out of the harbor and beach herself harmlessly somewhere along Brooklyn's Gravesend Bay, she floated directly toward disaster—the sixth and last tanker, the *Esso Brussels*. The 26,467-ton tanker, anchored low in the water, was carrying more than nine million gallons of a heavy oil known as Bunker C crude from Nigeria.

Powerless to do anything except blast a warning signal, Captain Patterson braced himself. Shortly before 1 A.M., the *Sea Witch* plowed into the *Esso Brussels*'s starboard side with a discordant grinding and grating of steel against steel. A large chunk of the freighter's bow was ripped off down almost to the waterline while the tanker sustained a twenty-foot gash and two ruptured holds, known as bladders, that contained oil. Within seconds, the impact ignited a horrific explosion and fireball.

Crew members aboard the tanker who survived the blast were slammed against bulkheads or jolted out of their bunks. Meanwhile, havoc reigned on the freighter. When its bow punctured the tanker's bladders, a raging river of burning oil poured onto the *Sea Witch* and headed for the stern, chasing her sailors down the deck.

Devastated by the accident, Captain Patterson watched helplessly from the bridge as his men ran for their lives or jumped overboard into the flaming water. Then he clutched his chest.

Half an hour earlier, John Buhler was standing in the pilothouse of the *Firefighter*, which was docked near the ferry terminal in St. George, Staten Island. Buhler, the chief engineer, was waxing poetic on the night with Matty Fitzsimmons, captain of the boat. "Boy, what a clear night," Buhler observed. "You can see all the way to Brooklyn."

Then Buhler went to his bunk and dozed off. But his sleep was cut short minutes later when the explosion from the collision reverberated across the harbor and jarred him awake. Like his fellow crewmen, he leaped to his feet and scampered topside to see what had happened. All eyes looked south at a massive tower of fire just north of the Verrazano-Narrows Bridge.

The *Sea Witch* Disaster

"It looks like a six-story building gone up all at once—except it's in the middle of the harbor," Buhler said to his crewmates. Within seconds, the *Firefighter* cast off and went to full throttle to chase down the blaze.

At 138 feet in length, the *Firefighter*, officially designated Fireboat 9, was the biggest vessel, the flagship, of New York's waterborne firefighting fleet. It carried eight high-pressure water cannon and a crew of ten: a captain, lieutenant, three engineers, and five firemen.

On this night, it would be the first emergency vessel to respond to one of the worst shipping fires in the city's history.

Buhler's hands tightened on the railing of the fireboat as it sliced through the water toward the blaze. "I've never seen so much fire in one place," he said in awe. He had been in the South Bronx when major fires were three-times-a-day events. But this blaze was extraordinary. Two ships, joined together by a tangled mass of steel, were burning from stem to stern and were drifting perilously straight toward the Verrazano-Narrows Bridge, which connects Staten Island with Brooklyn.

"I hope it doesn't get hung up on the bridge," Buhler said to Fitzsimmons. "If it hangs up on the pilings, it could destroy the bridge."

As the *Firefighter* neared the *Sea Witch*, the

burning freighter was rocked by a series of small explosions. "I hope we're not too close if it blows out of the water," Buhler said.

By now the current had pushed the two burning ships directly under the bridge's span, 228 feet above the water. Police on both sides of the bridge stopped vehicular traffic while flames from underneath were shooting so high that they scorched parts of the suspension bridge's superstructure. Fortunately, the ships didn't broadside any of the pilings and drifted past the bridge, causing it minimal damage.

The water around the two ships had turned into a glowing pond of fiery oil. The only way to fight the fire and rescue any surviving sailors was for Fitzsimmons to guide the *Firefighter* right into the blazing waters. If ever a fireboat could navigate through such hazardous waters, it was this one—a strong, steel-hulled ship with portholes more than an inch thick.

But there was still plenty of cause for concern. If the fiery water flared up while still surrounding the fireboat, it could suck all the oxygen out, suffocating everyone on board. It had happened before, years earlier, to a crew aboard a New York fireboat caught in the middle of a burning oil slick. All perished.

Another danger facing the *Firefighter*: The burning freighter could explode and sink and take the fireboat down with it.

The *Sea Witch* Disaster

Fitzsimmons expertly maneuvered the *Firefighter* into position to battle the blaze. While some of the crew aimed their water cannon at the fiery surface to keep the flames away from their boat, the others shot streams of water onto the burning vessels.

Below in the boiling hot engine room, where temperatures exceeded a brutal 125 degrees, Buhler tended to the pumps that were cranking out twenty thousand gallons of water a minute at high pressure for each of the *Firefighter's* eight cannon.

Buhler glanced out the portholes of the engine room to an unnerving sight—nothing but flames. "I hope the hull is strong enough to take this," he thought. Despite the intense heat below deck, Buhler didn't dare start the blowers that normally bring in cool air. He feared the blowers would suck in smoke and fumes from the burning fuel outside.

Up on deck the drama was playing out with a backdrop of flames. There had been no sign of any survivors on the *Sea Witch* until a firemen yelled, "I see a flashlight blinking at the stern!" Then another firefighter bellowed, "My God, look at all the people on the deck!"

The *Firefighter's* powerful searchlight cast its beam on thirty-two sailors clustered in the back waiting to be rescued before the flames killed them or the ship blew up. The fireboat moved down the starboard side of the burning hulk with all eight of its water cannons working at full capacity, firing steady streams on the flames. Down below, Buhler was told of the survivors, so he broke out bottles of water, blankets, first aid equipment, and other emergency provisions for their arrival.

As Fitzsimmons brought his boat along the stern of the burning freighter, his men set up a thirty-foot ladder that spanned the fiery water. The blaze on board the *Sea Witch* had advanced all the way to the stern, leaving the stranded sailors with only a few feet of deck that wasn't in flames.

Much to the bewilderment of the firefighters, the sailors refused to come down the ladder initially. "No, our captain comes first!" one of the sailors shouted down. "We're not leaving him behind."

Only then did the firemen learn that Captain William Patterson, who had tried so desperately to avoid a catastrophe, had collapsed from a heart attack and died moments after the collision. His loyal, grief-stricken crewmen had been carrying his body with them as they escaped from the advancing flames.

Firemen solemnly helped the sailors lower the captain's body onto the *Firefighter*'s deck. Then, in a matter of a few short minutes, the sailors, many of them blistered and oil-soaked, came down the ladder to safety. They were hustled below deck where Buhler gave them first aid and provisions.

The *Sea Witch* Disaster

By now all available fire, Coast Guard, and police boats were helping to douse the flames, search for survivors, or recover bodies. Meanwhile, the burning ships, still locked together in a fatal embrace, were drifting southeast toward Seagate, a private community on a peninsula near the famous Coney Island amusement park. Fire officials worried that if the vessels beached there, the flames could spread throughout the cherished old Brooklyn neighborhood. Fire trucks were dispatched to the area and took up defensive positions.

Fortunately, the burning vessels harmlessly ran aground about one thousand yards off the Brooklyn shore in Gravesend Bay.

As dawn broke, the fire on the *Esso Brussels* was brought under control. But the *Sea Witch* was still burning furiously, fueled in part by thousands of automobile tires in containers on the deck.

With the *Firefighter* and other fireboats training their water guns on the freighter, two tugs managed to pull the damaged vessels apart in less than ten minutes without incident. The worst was over. But there was still one more scare.

Seven firemen from Rescue 2, who had been ferried to the site by the fireboat, boarded the freighter to put out the last of the fires and search for victims. As the firemen stretched their hose lines and headed for the interior of the vessel, the *Sea Witch* suddenly listed hard to port and threatened to capsize right on top of the fireboat. Captain Fitzsimmons kept the boat close to the freighter while the men of Rescue 2 hurriedly abandoned ship and flew down the ladder to the deck of the *Firefighter*.

"All units stand off!" came the order over the fire radio. The fireboats moved away.

The ship righted herself and then heaved dangerously to starboard before righting herself again. After swaying a few more times, the *Sea Witch* stabilized, and the situation was declared under control by 7 A.M. The oil-stained, exhausted crewmen of the *Firefighter* were finally relieved early in the afternoon after toiling nonstop for twelve tense, grueling hours.

Of the sixty-three men aboard the *Sea Witch* and the *Esso Brussels,* sixteen sailors—nine from the tanker and seven from the freighter—died in the collision and ensuing fire. For rescuing thirty-two sailors and helping keep the burning tanker from blowing up, the *Firefighter* and her crew received the Gallant Ship Award from the Maritime Association.

As for the *Sea Witch,* two days after the collision, she was towed out to sea, where a Coast Guard cutter opened fire and sent the freighter to a watery grave.

WRONG WAY DOWN

The adrenalin was pumping throughout Chicago firefighter Jim Purl's body as he clambered up a 38-foot ladder toward a third-floor window of a burning hotel where a panic-stricken man was bellowing for help.

Aside from the fact that a man's life was at stake, Purl was especially eager because this was his first ladder rescue attempt. It turned out to be one of the strangest in Chicago firefighting history.

The brawny fireman from Squad 1 had wanted to do a ladder rescue for a long time. Even when he previously had worked on a tower ladder (one that has a basket and can rise up to 140 feet), he hadn't been in a situation where he needed to scale a ladder to save someone. But in the predawn hours of March 16, 1993, Purl finally got his chance—but it was nothing like he or his fellow firefighters had ever expected.

Purl had started his shift the day before by spending eight hours at the fire academy brushing up on rescue techniques. That evening he made one fire run—a rather odd one. He was called to a nearby fire station after a man walked in there asking for help in getting off a ring that was stuck on his finger. Purl used a special snipping tool to cut the ring. After returning to his fire station, Purl went to his sleeping quarters. Before dozing off, he thought about the parties he planned to attend during his upcoming day off in celebration of St. Patrick's Day.

Purl was jolted awake by a fire alarm that was called in at 4:02 A.M. He leaped out of his warm bed, donned his turnout gear, and hopped into the driver's seat of his squad's snorkel truck. The rig had a cherry picker-type ladder on top and was used to attempt rescues up to the fourth floor of a building.

The truck rolled down the ramp to the street and into a misty, chilly darkness where the temperature hovered in the thirties. Although the blaze was only a few blocks away, it still took longer than Purl liked. He had to navigate through narrow streets and tall buildings without speeding and he had to slow down at stoplights because it was difficult for anyone to see around the corners.

When he finally arrived at the Paxton Hotel on La Salle Avenue, he saw smoke billowing out of the windows but no flames. Residents and guests of the four-story hotel were leaning out of the upper windows, shouting for help and flailing their arms.

One person who seemed to be in the most immediate danger was a middle-aged man who was hanging halfway out of his window on the third floor where the smoke was the heaviest.

This is it, Purl thought. *I'm going to get my first ladder rescue. This guy is mine.*

Purl couldn't maneuver his rig close enough to the building because other fire trucks that had arrived first were blocking the way. So Purl and his fellow firefighters quickly extended a thirty-eight-foot fire ladder.

Within seconds, Purl scaled the ladder and reached the window where smoke was pouring out and the curtains were billowing.

"Get me out of here! For God's sake, save me!" pleaded the wild-eyed man, a longtime hotel resident whose name was Daniel Green. "And save my mother! She's inside too."

Purl peered into the smoke but it was too thick to see anyone else. He couldn't help Green immediately because a window air conditioner was in the way.

"Listen to me," Purl ordered him. "I need you to calm down. I'll get you out of there and then I'll go in and get your mother. But I need to get rid of this air conditioner first."

However, things didn't work out quite the way Purl had planned.

At six foot three and 220 pounds, Purl was a strong fireman. He would need every bit of his strength to pull off this rescue. As he braced himself against the ladder, he wrenched the air conditioning unit out of the window and tossed it away, creating an opening in the window large enough for Green to climb through.

"Let's go! Come on!" Purl yelled once he got the window cleared.

As Green emerged from the window, Purl saw how big Green was—about 260 pounds. *Well, at least I won't have to carry him down,* the fireman thought. But Purl wasn't prepared for what happened next.

The ladder was directly in front of the window and extended above the top of the frame. Instead of climbing out onto the ladder, Green, in his terrible fright, tried to go through it! He pushed his head between two rungs of the ladder and was now trying to get his beefy shoulders through, like a burglar attempting to squeeze into a much-too-small window.

"What are you doing?" Purl asked incredulously. "No, no. Go around to the side of the ladder!"

The firefighter gripped the rail of the ladder with one hand and tried to shove Green's head out from between the rungs. "You can't get through this way." But the more Purl pushed, the more the ladder pulled away from the building. *All I'm doing is pushing myself farther away from him,* Purl thought, looking down for a second to see several firefighters struggling mightily to keep the ladder from slipping.

Suddenly, the ladder started shifting to the left like the big hand on a clock going counterclockwise.

A little bit more and I'm going down three stories in full gear. I wonder what will happen to me?

"Sir, you're going the wrong way!" Purl hollered to Green. "You're going . . ." Purl gasped when he realized that smoke was coming from under Green's arms. *My gosh, no wonder the man is in a panic. His clothes are on fire.*

Purl needed to get Green out of there quickly not only to save the man's life but to clear the way for the firefighter to reach Green's mother, Velma, before she ended up overcome by smoke and flames. But Green was still taking the wrong route onto the ladder. Making the scene even more bizarre, he somehow became wrapped up in the curtains so it looked like he was wearing a dress.

Purl had managed to push Green's head out from between the rungs when the ladder began slipping further to the left.

"Oh, God, it's falling!" Purl shouted. He held onto the ladder, expecting to experience a horribly painful impact with the ground in a few seconds. But the ladder didn't fall. Miraculously, a rung had caught on a decorative brick that was sticking out from the building's façade. It was just long enough and strong enough to hold the ladder secure. And it kept the ladder close to the window so Green still had a chance to escape.

Whew, that was close, Purl said to himself. He glanced down at his fellow firefighters who were now doing all they could to keep the ladder from moving any more.

Meanwhile, Green climbed out of the window and, with his back to the smoke, grabbed hold of a ladder rail with his right hand and put his right foot on a rung. But he had trouble swinging his body onto the ladder. He wound up spread-eagled with his left hand and left leg hanging in the air. It was anybody's guess how long, or even if, he could hold on.

I've got to get him steady, Purl thought. While facing the building, the fireman stuck out his right leg, hooked it around Green's body and drew him toward the ladder. Green finally managed to get both hands and feet onto the ladder, although he was now practically on top of Purl.

Well, at least he's on the ladder, the fireman thought. "Okay, sir, get off of me. Then I can help you down."

Purl thought the worst was over. He was wrong, because the rescue turned into a wacky scene that belonged in a Buster Keaton flick.

Wrong Way Down

Somehow Green had managed to climb over Purl from the right side of the ladder to the left side and kept on going until he ended up on the wrong side. Mystifyingly, Green now had his back to the burning building, his hands gripping a rung from the underside of the ladder, his arms fully extended, and his legs dangling straight down. Facing him on the topside of the ladder was a totally dumbfounded Purl.

How in the world did that happen? Purl wondered. *He's done a three-sixty on me, and now he's trying to get down the wrong way. I can't believe this!*

But the fireman didn't have time to ponder the situation.

Green was attempting to move down the ladder without any kind of foothold, just one rung at a time, hand under hand like a kid on the monkey bars. *One slip and he's a goner,* Purl thought. *I've got to help him.*

With his chest pressed against the topside of the ladder, Purl reached down and grabbed Green's hips and thighs. Then Purl held on as he started to guide Green down, rung by rung. It was not ideal, but the firefighter could do little else for him.

The muscles in Purl's arms were beginning to quiver and sting because they were supporting most of Green's weight. Purl wanted to relax his arms for just a few seconds but he didn't dare. He knew that if he let go of Green, the man would not be able to hold on to the ladder and would fall to the pavement below.

I only hope I have the strength to get him safely to the bottom, Purl thought. He could feel the soreness increasing not only in his arms but also in the muscles in his chest.

He tried to think of something else to get his mind off the pain. His thoughts drifted to the old-timers from his former unit, Tower Ladder 10. *They always told me that carrying someone down a ladder was the hardest thing I would ever do, and they were right,* Purl told himself. *But I bet they never thought they'd see someone go down the ladder this way.*

Although Green was still gripping one rung at a time on his descent, virtually all his weight was being supported by Purl. As they passed by the second floor, Green moaned, "I can't hold on any longer. I just can't." His hands slipped off the rung.

Now Purl, gritting his teeth, was supporting all 260 pounds of Green's weight. It was too much to bear. Green slid out of Purl's sweaty grip and plunged the final ten feet to the pavement. He landed on his feet and then rolled over. Fortunately, he wasn't seriously hurt.

But Purl was. He scurried down the ladder and then doubled over with stomach cramps from muscles that he strained while trying to keep Green from falling. But Purl didn't have time to fret over his own pain.

"His mother is still up there," Purl said to fellow firefighter Tom Cavanaugh.

"Let's get her," said Cavanaugh.

"Okay, but let's try the stairs this time," Purl gasped.

The two men ran into the hotel lobby and did a double take. There, sitting at the reception desk was a young woman nonchalantly eating peanuts.

"She must think this is a movie," Purl said to Cavanaugh. Then to the desk clerk, he yelled out, "Where are the stairs?"

She pointed the way while still popping peanuts into her mouth.

Hoses stretched over the floor and other firefighters had already moved through the lobby to battle the flames on the upper floors, but still the young woman sat silently, munching her peanuts.

"She must be crazy," Purl said to Cavanaugh.

As Purl opened the door to the stairs, he was smacked by a solid wall of black smoke rolling down the steps. "We're never going to find that room with all this smoke," Cavanaugh said as Purl slammed the door to the stairwell shut.

"I guess we better go back to the ladder now," said Purl. Turning to the desk clerk, he shouted, "Hey, you. Get your register book and get the heck out of here."

When the two firemen reached the bottom of the ladder, Cavanaugh said, "I'll go up this time."

"No," said Purl. "This is my rescue. I really want to do this."

While climbing back up to the third floor to find Velma Green, he thought, *Maybe I should have picked another window when we first got here.*

When Purl reached the window, he was met with hot, thick smoke. He couldn't see anything inside and knew he was going to have to find the woman by getting down on his hands and knees and feeling his way around.

The fireman jumped into the open window, dropped to the floor, and started to crawl around feeling for Velma Green.

Outside, firefighter Steve Donovich stood in a basket of a tower ladder and maneuvered it until it was next to the window. Seeing Purl dive into the burning room, Donovich yelled to him, "Come on out! It's too dangerous in there!"

The heat and smoke were intense and Purl was about to give up when his hand touched flesh. "I found her! I found her!" Purl shouted.

Velma was unconscious and didn't appear to be breathing. But Purl still hoped that she was alive. He grabbed her limp body around the waist from the back so that she was folded over. Then he gave the 180-pound woman a bear hug and wrestled her toward the window.

Wrong Way Down

"I can't see you. Where are you?" Donovich yelled from his perch.

"I'm right here!" Purl shouted as loud as he could. "Just reach in."

Suddenly Purl saw Donovich's hands materialize in the smoke, snare the woman, and drag her over the windowsill and into the basket of the tower ladder.

"I'm coming too," Purl said and dove head first into the basket. Then the crowded basket was lowered to the ground, where waiting paramedics sprang into action.

"She's not breathing," Purl told them.

"She's in cardiac arrest," reported one of the paramedics as they put her on a gurney and ran with her to a waiting ambulance.

"I guess she's been in the smoke for a while," Purl told Cavanaugh. "I hope they can bring her back."

Purl didn't have time to worry about the woman.

"We need the snorkel in the back of the building," an officer said. "Hurry up. There are people we need to get out." While the single room occupancy hotel was only four stories tall, it was 150 feet deep and was much bigger than it looked from the outside.

The soot-covered firefighter slid into the driver's seat and eased the big truck through an alley next to the burning building. The space was so narrow he had to fold back the side mirrors to get through. Purl deftly backed up his big truck into a parking lot behind the building. Once in the lot, he sent up the snorkel's ladder.

Purl didn't do any more climbing. However, the firefighters of Squad 1 made more than a dozen other rescues before the blaze was brought under control four hours later. More than one hundred persons were saved by firefighters from all the companies. Tragically, nineteen people died in the fire. One of them was a man who filled a bathtub with water hoping to escape the flames. He was found boiled to death.

The next day Purl called the hospital and learned that Velma Green had been resuscitated in the ambulance and was going to make a full recovery. Her son Daniel, who sustained minor injuries, was with her.

For his actions, Purl received the Lambert Tree Award, the highest medal for valor given to Chicago firefighters. He accepted the award at a City Hall ceremony made all the more meaningful when Daniel and Velma Green came up and handed him a thank-you card for saving their lives.

"That's the greatest," Purl told them. "Usually you never hear from the people you save."

ARSON
AND
OLD LACE

All his life Tommy Russo had trained to fight fires. Now he was plotting to start one. But on this day, his plans had gone awry.

"It's as hot as a May day in here," Russo said, a little louder than he would normally talk. "Wow, it's stuffy. It's as hot as a May day in here."

The reference to "May day" was supposed to bring cops and fire marshals smashing through the door of the Brooklyn apartment where he and three arsonists were discussing a job. But the cavalry didn't come.

Russo, thirty-six, a veteran fire marshal, was working undercover as a mobster. He was trying to nail an experienced, professional firebug named "Rabbit" and some of his fellow torches. Rabbit, whose real name was L. G. Clark, didn't know his new Mafia pal was a really a fire investigator trying to squelch a wave of blazes that was turning the Bedford-Stuyvesant neighborhood into a collection of empty lots.

Why don't they come? Maybe this wire isn't working. Russo thought, trying to keep his cool as he glanced at the three arsonists in the dimly lit ground-floor apartment.

One of the torches started getting mean. Staring at Russo, he snarled, "How do I know you're not a cop? I think you're a pile of bullshit!" He wasn't that big, maybe five foot ten, but he had been smoking pot and taking some other drug, so he was in a menacing mood.

Oh, damn, something bad is going to happen, thought the strapping six-foot fire marshal. "It's as hot as a May day in here," he said one more time. He wondered if the train that was rumbling by on the elevated tracks outside the apartment building was screwing up the transmission or if the radio transmitter taped under his armpit was working at all.

Just then Rabbit's buddy pulled a hooked carpet knife from his shirt and pressed it against Russo's throat. *This is it,* Russo told himself. *I'm either going to die here or bluff him out. This cowboy is high on something and he doesn't like white guys.*

Russo had grown up near President Street in Brooklyn, a neighborhood that had produced the cream of the current generation of Mafia dons and capos. He had learned not to take any guff on the street when he was a kid. *This is the time to use your South Brooklyn routine,* Russo thought. *If he uses that knife on me, that will have to be the way it goes. But I'm not going stand here and take his shit. The hell with that blade.* So Russo let loose with a barrage of expletives that could have peeled the paint from walls.

While Russo fired his salvo of vulgarity, Rabbit started pleading with the knife wielder. "Hey, man, he's okay. He's a friend of Nat Davis, man. He's Mafiosi and he's gonna give us a whole lot of work. Man, don't hurt him, he's money to us."

I love Rabbit's loyalty and fast mouth, Russo thought, *but I can't wait to put him in jail. I only hope I live to do it.*

Then, as fast as the razor-edged fury had begun, it ended. The knife went back into the shirt of the angry arsonist, who turned his back, folded his arms, and stomped off to the other end of the room.

"Hey, look, if you dudes don't want to work with me I can find somebody else," Russo snapped, hoping he had hidden from them how scared he was and praying he would never be this scared again. But he was angry, too, because of the lack of response from the backup team of the District Attorney squad detectives who were parked in a van outside the apartment.

"Let's go," Russo said to Rabbit. Turning to the others, he said, "If you guys can calm down and not act like shits, we can meet again in a couple of days and talk serious business."

Later, after he and Rabbit split, Russo found out that the radio transmitter he was wearing worked only intermittently. But the tape recorder he carried caught the whole conversation. He felt good knowing that the authorities would have enough evidence to arrest Rabbit and his pals. But the timing wasn't right yet.

Russo had bigger fish to fry in this case, a dangerous yet ludicrous case that became known as the "Arson and Old Lace Caper."

In 1975, the experienced fire investigator had just finished an eighteen-month stint in Manhattan working undercover in sleazy dives in the then-notorious Times Square area. He cracked a case involving rival Mafia crews who had been throwing Molotov cocktails to set fire to each other's hooker joints.

Following his success with that case, Russo was loaned to the Queens District Attorney's detective squad. He was called into a meeting with several fire marshals, detectives, and Assistant District Attorney Geraldine Ferraro, who would later become the Democratic Party's Vice Presidential nominee in 1984. They wanted him involved in a new investigation that was as serious as it was incongruous.

Two grandmothers were suspected of fleecing insurance companies out of millions of dollars by running an arson ring that had turned hundreds of insured houses and businesses into charred ruins.

Real estate brokers Rose Shiffman, seventy-three, and her sister Sylvia Goldberg, sixty-six, and Shiffman's son, Abraham Jack Shiffman, a lawyer, had been buying up houses and shorefront buildings in Queens since 1965. It appeared that virtually all the properties they owned were highly flammable, because they burned to the ground. In ten years, nobody had ever been able to lay a glove on them with a criminal complaint. Rumor in the D.A.'s squad was that the three of them had political pull and were hooked up with other real estate agents and lawyers who were using matches to make profits on the insurance of their unwanted property.

Investigators scored a huge break when Nat Davis, a torch extraordinaire, squealed. Davis was responsible for setting dozens of fires himself and had been acting as an executive firebug for crooked lawyers and real estate brokers. He was the person who set up the jobs and hired the arsonists who would actually light the matches.

He and his fellow torches were a virtual firestorm in the Rockaways, a beachfront strip in southern Queens where wood-frame bungalows and old Victorian resort hotels were bursting into flames on a regular basis.

But then Davis, a balding, short man who would never think to muscle anybody, was convicted on a gun charge and sent to an upstate prison. He didn't like the cold winter weather there. He didn't like the food there. He didn't like his fellow convicts there. So Davis sent a message to the Queens District Attorney: "If you get me out of here, I'll talk. I'll give you the people who paid me." He was willing to tell investigators all about an arson gang run by a couple of grandmothers, respected members of the community, who were responsible for dozens, maybe hundreds, of fires in Queens, Brooklyn, and upstate New York.

The D.A. signed Davis out of prison and brought him to the courthouse office to meet with the arson task force. As the new kid on the block, Russo listened intently as the District Attorney squad detectives talked with Davis about a game plan.

"We need to come up with an undercover guy, somebody who Nat here can introduce as a reliable torch," said a detective.

"Yeah, that would work," said Russo, who didn't readily volunteer for the job because he had just emerged from a lengthy, dangerous undercover assignment.

Arson and Old Lace

After an hour or two, Davis agreed that he would go to his main contact, lawyer Jack Shiffman, and introduce the bogus torch to him. "I'll say I'm out of jail on a technicality and I'm too hot to do any work myself. Shiffman and the old ladies will buy that from me. We go way back."

"Okay, so who's it gonna be?" asked one detective, staring right at Russo. Suddenly Russo realized everybody was looking at him.

Almost immediately he had a new persona— Tommy Cerillo, a Mafia hood with a talent for lighting matches. If needed, a detective would pose as his boss, a mob capo, to make the masquerade look authentic.

So Davis made the rounds of his old clientele to tell them he was back in business, but only as an agent for Cerillo, a new up-and-coming professional fire starter. A few days after the game plan was set, Russo, as Cerillo, was walking with Davis to meet Jack Shiffman at the lawyer's office. Russo and Davis were wired, wearing tape recorders and radio transmitters. Shiffman, who said he had some business for Davis, was suspicious when the arsonist brought along a stranger.

This guy smells a rat, Russo thought. *He's not going to go for somebody he doesn't know. He's too smart.*

Russo was right. After much wrangling over his

involvement in the next torch job, Shiffman agreed to send Cerillo over to meet his mother and his aunt for their impressions of this new firebug. *What a nice boy,* Russo thought. *He puts his mother up front and with his dear old auntie, too.*

Russo and Davis went to Rose Shiffman's high-rise apartment to meet her and Sylvia Goldberg. The old ladies weren't impressed. Pointing to Russo, Rose asked Davis, "So who is he? I don't know this guy. Are you sure he's all right? Why can't you do it for me?"

"I'm too hot now, so I can't work for you anymore," Davis explained. "But I got you this guy who can do the job for you. Tommy Cerillo is the best. He's Italian from South Brooklyn."

Russo watched the exchange with bemusement. Then he studied the features of the elderly women. *These two old broads look like they've lived their whole life on a beach. Their skin is like tanned leather—brown, tough, and well oiled.*

Davis kept up his sales pitch for "Cerillo" until he finally wore down their resistance. "I know him a long time," Davis lied. "I've worked with Tommy in the past, and I assure you, he's fine."

"Cerillo" joined in to toot his own horn. "Look, I got plenty of work. I don't need this. You don't trust me, I'm outta here. Right now." He started to get up.

"Now, now, Mr. Cerillo, don't get upset," Rose

said, putting a grandmotherly hand on his arm. "I have to talk to some people first and then we can do business."

The sweet old ladies served the two arsonists tea and cookies and arranged for another meeting.

Three days later Russo met Sylvia Goldberg in a strip mall parking lot to talk about burning down a beach house in the Bayswater section of Queens. He had parked in a spot that was in perfect view of a camera concealed in a nearby van operated by the District Attorney's detective team. Russo's car was wired to catch every word exchanged between the real estate agent and the undercover fire marshal.

"Look, this will cost you $2,000," he told her. "I get $500 before I even see the building and $1,500 after it burns. That's the deal. You can take it or leave it."

"I know what the deal is, Mr. Cerillo," said Sylvia. "I wasn't born yesterday. I have the money right here in my bag."

"Okay, then take it out and let's count it to make sure we're both honest."

Sylvia pulled out a pile of bills from her purse and counted out $500 and handed it to him. "It would be nice if you could burn it tonight," she said.

Oh, boy, we got her big time now, Russo thought, hoping the woman would think his smile was prompted by the money she gave him.

"Let's go take a look at the place," she said. "We'll take my car. It's more comfortable."

As the two headed off to the scene of the would-be crime in her new Cadillac, he thought, *What a wrinkled old broad. I wonder how many bottles of suntan lotion she uses in a year.* He was aware that when the fire-loving granny wasn't in Queens arranging for the burning down of houses, she and her firebug sister were on a beach in Florida soaking up the rays.

The house she wanted torched was an ordinary two-story, one-family wood frame home built on a concrete slab right on the beach. *Why does she want to torch this place?* Russo wondered. *This is about as nice as my house on Long Island.*

Sylvia answered the question so quick Russo thought for a moment he had asked out loud. "It's been on the market for months and I can't get my price," she explained. "I can't sell it and I don't want to let it go at a loss."

She took him inside. The place had a garage and a boiler-utilities room on the ground floor. The second floor contained the kitchen, living room, and bedrooms.

"Gee, it's not a bad house," Russo observed as they entered the kitchen. "Are those new cabinets?"

"You bet," she replied. "I put them in a couple of months ago to make the kitchen look better, but they didn't help."

"Gee, it's a shame to burn new cabinets."

"Are you married?"

"Yes."

"Do you have a house?"

"Yes."

"So you take the kitchen cabinets out and bring them to your house before you set the fire. That way they won't go to waste and you'll get a bonus," Sylvia said with a smile and a nod.

"If you do this job for me, I'll send you all over the country to burn. You'll make a lot of money and never be out of work."

As they walked back outside, she added, "Now don't forget to take the cabinets. It'll make your wife happy. It would be nice if you burn this place down tonight."

"I don't know," Russo said, trying to stall. "There's another house right next door, not even fifteen feet away. I don't want that house to burn and maybe kill somebody."

"Don't worry about that," she said reassuringly. "The wind is always blowing so that the fire will go away from the neighbors."

Sylvia then drove him back to his car. After he left her, Russo thought, *We have the evidence we need to nail Sylvia and her sister and we'll get her nephew, the lawyer, too.* But arrests weren't imminent. Not yet. He knew his bosses would want him to arrange for Sylvia to send him all over the country where he could pile up evidence against other people involved with the Arson and Old Lace Gang. But to do that, he would have to prove to the crooks that he was a dependable arsonist. *I wonder if I can set fire to that house to keep this investigation moving forward.*

"No way. If you light a fire, we'll have to arrest you," declared a legal expert in the D.A.'s office after scouring law books searching for a legal loophole that Russo could use to keep the gang from getting suspicious. That meant Russo had to stall the crooks while casting a wider net for other firebugs in the gang.

The day after Russo's meeting with Sylvia, he and Davis, who were each wearing a wire, visited Jack Shiffman again at his office. When he learned that the beach house hadn't been burned down yet, he became angry and ordered the two men out.

"From now on, you deal with my mother," he told them. "I don't want any more to do with this. I don't like the way you guys are working."

"Cerillo" then visited Rose, who gave him a cup of tea and a piece of kichel, a pastry. "As soon as you burn down the beach house I'll give you a job upstate," she told him. "I'll get you big money, commercial buildings, really big things. Now be good and burn the house for me."

Arson and Old Lace

During the investigation, Russo learned from Davis, Rose, and Sylvia that the gang was larger than he realized. Davis introduced him to L. G. "Rabbit" Clark, an arsonist who had been lighting a lot of matches in Brooklyn with some of his cronies.

That's how Russo ended up in a Bedford-Stuyvesant apartment with a knife at his throat. He had been talking to Rabbit and his arson pals about working with them on future jobs.

But when the beach house still hadn't burned down, Rabbit became suspicious. He and his cohorts were getting set to burn several buildings in Brooklyn, but Rabbit wasn't sure he could trust his new Mafia pal. So "Cerillo" invited him to have an Italian dinner on Brooklyn's President Street, a well-known mob neighborhood, with "Capo Bobo Sinise," played by an undercover Queens detective. The ruse was part of a plan to take down the arsonist and his fire-starting buddies before they had a chance to torch any more buildings.

At the dinner, Russo and the detective, both wearing wires, played their roles to perfection. Rabbit was duly impressed by the "mobsters." When they finished their meal, Russo thought, *This guy thinks he's got a part in "The Godfather in Brooklyn."*

As the three men left the restaurant in their cars, they were quickly blocked by a swarm of police. Cops yanked open the car doors and wrenched the men out. "Cerillo" was slammed facedown on the hood. Rabbit was treated more gently so he could watch the cops pull an "illegal" gun out of "Cerillo's" pocket and announce they were sending the "mobster" back to the Bronx, where he was wanted on a murder rap.

Rabbit, who was carrying an illegal knife, was sent to Central Booking to await arraignment in the morning.

The next day, while Rabbit was being arraigned in open court on the minor weapons charge, his public defender asked, "Where's the other suspect?"

A Brooklyn detective witlessly answered, "There isn't any. The other suspect is an undercover fire marshal."

Rabbit was stunned by the revelation and soon spread the word on the street that "Tommy Cerillo" was a plant.

Russo didn't know it at the time, but his life was now in danger big time. Only fate saved him. Another fire marshal happened to be in court on an unrelated case, saw what happened, and ran for the phone to alert the D.A.

When Russo arrived at headquarters, his supervisor told him, "Your cover is blown. We're putting a guard on your house. Get your wife and kids to stay somewhere else for a while."

"I guess I'm finished in Brooklyn," Russo said.

Arson and Old Lace

Thanks to Russo's undercover work, the Arson and Old Lace Gang was broken up. Rose Shiffman, Jack Shiffman, and Sylvia Goldberg were arrested on a variety of arson and fraud charges. Rabbit and his fellow firebugs, including the doper with the carpet knife, were slapped with a slew of arson charges. But a bigger school of fish swam away because Russo's undercover job was cut short by a detective's careless remark.

"No more undercover work, please," Russo told his boss after the case ended and he and his family were able to return to their Long Island home. His supervisor agreed.

After having a knife to his throat, Russo figured his next assignment would be much safer. He was wrong.

Starting a new anti-arson program, he and partner Ralph Granielo hooked up with city detectives in the South Bronx, where they patrolled neighborhoods such as the notorious Fort Apache area. Their job was to prevent fires by collaring people who looked suspicious and were hanging around abandoned buildings.

It was 1975, an unusually fiery year in the borough. People were torching their own apartments in run-down buildings so the city would give them new apartments or emergency grants up to $2,000 for new clothes and furniture.

Cruising the blocks with an army of officers and fire marshals aimed at stopping arson proved to be a big success. Russo and Granielo would roust druggies, hookers, and squatters from abandoned premises. The fire marshals would stop and search anyone who was carrying a suspicious package and loitering near a building.

What turned out to be Russo's last case began July 7, 1975, a hot day in a hot neighborhood.

He and his partner and two plainclothes cops were in a car together looking for suspicious characters when Russo spotted two men, one of whom was carrying a large brown paper bag, walking near an abandoned apartment building on St. Ann's Avenue. "Stop these guys," Russo ordered. "I don't like the look of the package the big one is carrying."

The car screeched to a stop and the lawmen piled out and chased after the suspects. Russo nabbed the smaller man, Ralph Lanzot, while the other three took off after the bigger one with the bag.

"Don't hurt me, don't hurt me!" pleaded Lanzot.

Russo knew the neighborhood was a powder keg of anti-cop feeling so he ordered Lanzot to get inside the empty building. *I better get this guy in a place where he can't be seen before we get a crowd and I have to shoot my way out,* Russo told himself.

Once inside the lobby, the suspect confessed, "Look, I got a knife in my back pocket."

Arson and Old Lace

Russo, his .38 detective special still in his waistband holster, nodded. "Take it out slowly and let it drop." His eyes followed the knife as Lanzot pulled it out of his pocket and dropped it. Russo watched the knife clank and bounce on the tile floor.

But when he looked up, he saw a gun pointed at his face. *Where the hell did that come from?* he thought. He realized Lanzot had played him for a sucker, giving up the knife, acting scared, and waiting for a chance to pull his own four-inch-barreled .38. *What a dope, dope, dope I am. I didn't frisk him. I let him con me into thinking he was a harmless guy. I'm here all alone and my gun is still stuck in my holster.*

"Give me your gun, man, and then let's go down the hall, " Lanzot snarled.

"I'll give you the gun, but I'm not going anywhere," Russo replied with a lot more bravado than he felt. He handed his gun to Lanzot. "If you're going to shoot me, do it here so my partners can hear it and shoot your ass off before you get away."

Perplexed over what to do now, Lanzot didn't move, but kept his weapon trained on Russo's head.

Seeing the suspect's eyes darting back and forth, Russo thought, *He's going to run. I think I'll get out of this alive.* He was right.

In a flash, Lanzot bolted out the door. Russo immediately called in a "10-13"—the radio signal that a law officer is in immediate danger and needs help fast. Within minutes, cars from the Fort Apache and neighboring precincts flooded the area with cops, but Lanzot escaped with the fire marshal's gun. Lanzot's companion also slipped through the dragnet after dropping the brown paper bag. Inside the bag cops found a loaded Luger pistol.

I'm going to catch hell for this, Russo thought, lamenting the loss of his gun. *The boss has every right to be pissed. This is how you get killed, because you wait for the other guy to do something bad before you react. Next time, no more Mr. Nice Guy.*

Feeling miserable over the incident, he spent the rest of the day filling out paperwork concerning his missing pistol.

Stealing a police weapon was an affront to any cop and fire marshal in the city. The word went out on the street that every hooker, petty dope dealer, and car thief was going to be stopped for questioning until the gun was recovered.

Three days later, an anonymous tipster phoned saying the gun was in a dumpster on St. Ann's Avenue. Russo found the dumpster and, with his bemused partner looking on, picked through the trash heap for his .38. "I feel like a Class A dope," Russo muttered to Granielo.

Adding to the indignity, the neighborhood kids, who apparently knew the location of the gun, made a game of it. "No, no, you're getting cold," the kids giggled as the chagrined fire marshal rummaged through one side of the dumpster. When he sifted trash on the other side, they said, "Yeah, that's better. You're getting red hot now."

After he found his weapon, Russo devoted the next few days to hunting for Lanzot. Russo was scheduled to go on vacation July 12, a Saturday, but put it off one day so he had more time to track him down.

"I want this guy really bad," Russo told Granielo. They received a tip that Lanzot was hanging around his girlfriend's apartment, so the fire marshals paid her a visit. "Ralphie ain't here," she told them. However, she agreed to let them search the place.

In the bedroom, Granielo opened the closet door and found Lanzot, clad in only his undershorts, crouched inside and pointing his big .38 at them.

"Drop the gun!" Granielo and Russo yelled at the same time. They repeated their order but Lanzot didn't move. Granielo, who was only two feet from the gunman, reached down to grab the weapon. Suddenly, Lanzot fired his gun once, twice, three times.

Oh, jeez, he got Ralph! Russo thought, watching his partner fall. Russo fired twice and retreated to the bedroom door. Then he fired two more times before advancing toward the closet. *I don't know if I hit him, maybe I did.*

Not hearing any movement coming from inside the closet, Russo cautiously stepped closer. All of a sudden a bullet ripped through his jaw with the blow of a sledgehammer, knocking his senses out of whack, except for the pain he felt.

He didn't hear a thing. Everything appeared to him in slow motion, his gun falling out of his hand, his knees buckling, his body crashing to the floor, even the dust floating up from the impact when he hit the floor. It all seemed to take minutes.

When he regained his senses seconds later, he looked up and straight into the barrel of Lanzot's pistol. *He's going to give me another cap,* Russo thought. *I wonder if I'll feel it.*

Just then Mike DiMarco, a member of his backup team, rushed into the room. Lanzot aimed his gun at him and then back to Russo. "Don't hurt them anymore!" DiMarco shouted. "I'll move back and you can run for it. Just don't shoot!"

As DiMarco stepped out of the apartment, Lanzot grabbed the gun of the fallen Granielo and sprinted out the door and up a stairway to the building's roof.

Dazed and bleeding from the side of his face, Russo staggered to his feet. His jaw was shattered, shot off its hinges and dangling down to his collar bone. Clutching his pistol, he checked on his partner, who was sprawled on the floor unable to move. Then Russo wobbled to the window and tried to shout to two detectives outside. He made a guttural sound like a wounded bear. Seeing the horror on their faces when they spotted him, he thought, *I must sound really horrible and look even worse.*

Russo took the yellow wristband he was wearing, which identified him to cops as an undercover fire marshal, and put it around his head so it would be visible to the police who were arriving at the scene. Then he went after Lanzot, who had left behind a trail of blood. As Russo entered the hallway, he encountered several cops with their guns drawn and aimed at him. But, seeing the yellow band on Russo's head, they hesitated to fire. Then DiMarco came running down the hall, shouting, "Don't shoot him! He's one of ours!"

By now Lanzot had made it to the roof of the apartment, tailed by three detectives who quickly had him cornered. But he refused to give up. Blasting away with both guns, he triggered a wild shootout that ended only after he had been shot five times.

Lanzot recovered from his wounds, was convicted of several felonies, and sent to prison.

Granielo suffered a serious injury. The only bullet that hit him fragmented when it struck a bone in his shoulder and cut his spine, paralyzing him from the waist down. The strong-minded fire marshal eventually returned to the fire department, but in a wheelchair. He rose in the ranks to become a

Deputy Chief and was affectionately known as "Chief Ironsides."

Russo needed five operations and several other medical and dental procedures to rebuild his face and mouth. But he felt lucky. Doctors told him a piece of the bullet had scraped the lining of his carotid artery, and but for a fraction of a fraction of an inch, he would have bled to death.

After he recovered, Russo decided his fire marshal days were over. He started his own business investigating blazes for insurance companies. An expert on the way buildings structurally react to fire, he was hired to work with federal authorities to determine how the World Trade Center towers collapsed.

But no matter how big his cases are today, Tommy Russo can never forget the Arson and Old Lace Gang and Ralph Lanzot.

THE GRIP OF LIFE

Numerous officers down!" screamed the frantic voice over the emergency scanner. "I repeat. Numerous officers down! We need medical help fast!"

More than a dozen FBI agents and other law enforcement officers were engaged in a fierce gun battle with two murderers in a side street in Miami while the dead and the wounded lay sprawled on the ground.

Hearing the gripping news from the scanner in his office at the airport, medic Charlie Perez of the Miami Dade Fire Rescue Department's new Air Rescue chopper turned to pilot Billy Riggs and shouted, "We've got to get this helicopter up now!"

The problem was that the helicopter, a six-passenger Stretch Ranger, was not equipped for medical evacuations. It was on loan to the department while its new, big, powerful air rescue chopper was in the shop being fitted as an airborne emergency room. The copter at the helipad was just a training ship.

"It's not ready," Riggs declared. "We're not equipped."

"It doesn't matter," Perez retorted. Lawmen were dying in the street and they needed medical help now. "I'll grab some gear and we'll go."

Riggs, Perez, and two fellow paramedics sprinted toward the helicopter. Whether or not they were ready, they were going. On April 11, 1986, the department's air rescue unit was about to make its "mass casualty" debut—a literal baptism under fire because they were about to drop into a hail of bullets.

An elite FBI squad working out of the Miami field office had spent months trying to capture two murderous men, William Russell Matix and Michael Platt, who had pulled off nine bank robberies in less than a year. The dangerous duo was also suspected in at least three murders, two of which were their wives. One woman had been found bound, gagged, and stabbed several times. The other had been shot in the mouth.

The criminals were armed with an arsenal that included a 12-gauge shotgun, .357 magnum pistols, and an assault rifle with a large capacity magazine and five thousand rounds of ammunition.

The Grip of Life

Unlike a lot of criminals, they knew how to use the weaponry because they were former U.S. Army Rangers who had met while serving in Korea.

The agents were getting more fervent in their efforts to nab the gunmen as the robbers became bolder. In the last two holdups, Matix and Platt had hit the same bank using the same getaway car. They didn't even bother to change the license plates.

Relying on a tip from a gutsy citizen, the Miami FBI office put a fourteen-man squad, including two SWAT-team-qualified agents, on the streets in ten vehicles to cruise South Dixie Highway where the outlaws were expected to strike again. The FBI knew Matix and Platt were career criminals who were armed to the teeth and willing to die rather than be caught.

The feds were looking for a black 1982 Chevy that had been carjacked, its owner murdered in cold blood. Just after 9 A.M. a federal agent spotted the Chevy and tailed it. Inside the Chevy were Matix and Platt, who immediately became suspicious. They started making right turns to confirm that they were being followed. When they decided they had been recognized, the Chevy sped off. Within seconds, three federal agents' cars were in pursuit.

After that, everything went wrong for the feds. Knowing reinforcements were moving in fast, the agents in the three chase cars tried to force the gunmen off the road on Southwest 82nd Avenue in a quiet neighborhood. What resulted was a four-car crack-up that injured several lawmen. The impact from the crash knocked the pistol out of the hand of the squad's sharpshooter and sent it under a seat where he couldn't find it. Another agent lost his glasses and was unable to see well enough to shoot.

After the wreck, Matix and Platt grabbed their weapons and moved right into combat mode. They bolted out of their smashed car with guns blazing and killed two federal agents. From then on, it was a confusing, brutal firefight to the death with shotguns, magnums, and assault rifles spraying hundreds of bullets, shattering the neighborhood tranquility and sending alarmed citizens diving for cover.

Meanwhile, back at the heliport, Perez jumped into the copilot's seat of the chopper with his medical bags while his two partners hopped aboard. Riggs, an old-time helicopter instructor who had seen it all from Vietnam to Florida, looked at Perez and said, "I don't know if this bird will take the weight of all the wounded."

"We'll worry about that later," Perez replied. "We just got to get there as fast as we can."

None of the four said anything during the five-minute flight to the battle zone. They just listened to the shaken voices of FBI agents and police officers coming over the radio. In the background, Perez could hear bursts of gunfire and the wailing of sirens as the voices grew more edgy.

"We've exchanged nine or ten shots!"

"Another officer down!"

"We need medical attention pronto!"

Moments later, the improvised rescue helicopter swooped and circled over the wild scene of what would go down as one of the bloodiest gun battles in FBI history. Men hiding behind trees and wrecked cars were firing at each other as cop cars and ambulances converged to the combat zone.

"This looks like something out of a movie," Perez said to Riggs. "There are bodies all around." The roar of the copter's engine drowned out his words. "I can see men with guns. You can't tell who's who."

Below, members of a Miami Dade County Fire Department emergency unit were caught in the line of fire, but they still feverishly worked on an officer who was critically wounded. They were trying to stabilize him before rushing him to the ambulance.

"We've got to get down there fast!" Perez told Riggs. "They need our help."

"The place is jammed, there's no place to land," Riggs replied. "Too many police and emergency cars." Then he spotted a nearby three-story parking garage and smoothly lowered his chopper so Perez and the two other paramedics could jump out onto the roof.

Perez and his two partners pounded down the garage stairs, still hearing the sounds of gunfire. At the garage entrance, they paused for a moment, trying to figure out what was happening and where they should go.

In front of Perez, bullets whizzed back and forth. Men lay on the street in pools of blood. Angry shouts and anguished cries filled the air.

God, look at those bodies. There're all over the place, he thought. Then it dawned on him. *I'm not wearing a bulletproof vest. None of us are.* But that wasn't going to stop them from doing their job, which was tending to the wounded men no matter what.

Perez took a deep breath, then he and his partners split up and dashed into the battlefield. He ran over to a medic from Rescue 23, another Miami fire unit, who was working furiously on an FBI agent who was bleeding from several gunshot wounds. "We're going to move him now," the medic said. "We're set to get him to the hospital by ambulance. But there are other men, some in bad shape, who're going to need air transport. They're most likely going to die if they don't get help quickly."

In addition to fatally shooting two agents, Matix and Platt had seriously wounded five other lawmen, including special agent Edmundo Mireles Jr., whose left arm was riddled with bullets. After shooting him, the two killers scrambled back into their wrecked but drivable car and tried to run over another agent and escape.

Despite the blood gushing from his now useless left arm, Mireles, who was close to blacking out, managed to blast both the driver and passenger, painfully working the slide action of his shotgun with his right hand to get a fresh shell in the chamber. He kept firing until both gunmen were wounded and his 12-gauge was out of shells. Although weakened by a severe loss of blood, Mireles drew his service revolver and staggered toward the car, his gun blazing. Bleeding badly themselves, Platt and Matix returned fire but missed him. Before they had a chance to reload and kill him, they died in a salvo of bullets from advancing lawmen. Mireles didn't see them die. He had already collapsed in the street.

At first, Perez didn't notice Mireles. Perez had gone up to the open window of the killers' car and saw Platt slumped over the wheel, his head and body honeycombed with bullet holes. *He's DOA, boy is he DOA,* Perez thought.

Just then a cop ran up to him and yelled, "He's one of the bad guys. Leave him. We've got an FBI agent who needs your help right now."

With one hand on Perez' arm, the police officer hustled him over to Mireles, whose left arm was spurting blood profusely. Perez could quickly tell that a bullet had hit an artery, causing Mireles to hemorrhage.

He's going to bleed to death if I don't move fast, Perez told himself. He wasn't about to waste time putting on a tourniquet. Instead, he relied on the strength of his bare hands to keep the life from oozing out of the wounded FBI agent. So he clamped his hands around Mireles's arm above the wound to stem the flow of blood. *My God, I'm holding this guy's life in my hands,* Perez thought.

As he kneeled on the street gripping Mireles's arm, Perez noticed an eerie silence. "Thank God, the gunfire has stopped," he said to the policeman standing over them.

"Don't relax yet," the cop answered. "There might still be some more bad guys around here." Fortunately there weren't.

A few yards away, he saw his two partners bent over another fallen agent who was writhing in pain from being shot. "How bad is he?" Perez asked them.

"Bad. He's lost a lot of blood."

"We've got to get these guys out by chopper," Perez declared. "We're running out of time!"

With the assistance of another medic, Perez helped the barely conscious Mireles to his feet and draped his arms over their shoulders. Together they half carried, half dragged the federal agent toward the parking garage. But Perez kept an iron grip on the agent's bleeding arm. Meanwhile, Perez's partners were behind him, carrying their seriously wounded agent.

On the way there, Mireles, in shock and becoming disoriented, began to cry and tried to pull away. The anguished federal agent moaned, "I can't believe it happened. My partner was killed. I can't believe this."

"Okay, try to stay calm," Perez told him. "We're going to get you to a hospital real soon," said Perez. His fingers and wrists were beginning to ache from clutching Mireles so hard, but the firefighter wasn't about to loosen his grasp.

I could lose him any minute, Perez fretted to himself. *He could bleed to death if he yanks free from me. If I can keep him calm for three to four minutes, it should be enough time to get him in the chopper and to the hospital. I can do this. I'll get him there.*

With the agent's feet hardly touching the steps, Perez and his fellow medic hauled him up three flights of stairs to the roof of the parking garage. Perez's hands were sticky with blood and growing tired from squeezing Mireles's arm.

As they reached the helicopter, Perez reassured him, "You're going to be okay. You're going to make it." But Mireles, who was still in shock, kept repeating, "I can't believe it. My partner is gone. My partner is dead."

After Mireles and the other seriously wounded

agent were put aboard and the paramedics climbed in, the helicopter lifted off. Perez took one last look at the scene of the carnage below him—the wrecked cars, the blood in the streets, and Platt slumped over the wheel of the black Chevy. About a hundred yards away, a paramedic team was working on a downed lawman. *This is a day I'll never forget,* Perez said to himself.

He continued to keep his hands clamped on the agent's bleeding arm. At the same time, he called into Baptist Hospital over the radio: "We're coming in with two injured agents. We'll arrive in three or four minutes. Their vital signs are stable."

During the flight, Mireles was still talking and still agitated, although he was growing weaker every second. He kept mumbling repeatedly, as if in a trance, "My partner is dead. I can't believe it."

Moments later, the helicopter touched down at the hospital's helipad near the emergency room. "Everything's going to be all right now," said Perez, still putting pressure on the agent's arm. Doctors and nurses with IV bottles and gurneys quickly whisked the bleeding FBI agents away to the ER where surgeons treated the bullet-savaged victims. They and their wounded colleagues eventually recovered and returned to duty.

In seconds, it was all over for the air rescue team. The four men sat in the idling helicopter and tried to catch their breath while going over in their minds the frightening and deadly gunfight that had played out in the past half hour.

Before Perez could think any more, Riggs shouted, "We're going up." The helicopter lifted off again and headed back to the scene of the shootings.

"Try to rest and get your head together," Perez told the other paramedics. "We'll be there in under five minutes." Only then did Perez feel the tension go out of his hands that helped save the life of the wounded FBI man.

Back over the site, Perez said to Riggs, "Let's circle a little and see where we can do the most good." Then Perez radioed the site commander, asking for orders.

"It's okay," the commander replied. "We have plenty of people here treating the wounded and nobody needs to be moved by air. You guys can go home. Nice job and thanks."

"*De nada*," answered Perez in Spanish. "Forget it."

SMOKY JOE

On the breezy afternoon of June 15, 1922, a cigarette carelessly tossed by a carpenter triggered a massive fire that raged through rows of frame houses in the beachfront town of Arverne, New York.

Strong ocean winds from the northeast fanned the flames, spreading them rapidly from one wood structure to the next. The town's firefighting apparatus, three fire trucks, were late in responding because earlier they had been dispatched to fight a small fire in an old summerhouse northeast of town.

As a result of the delay in responding to the fire at Arverne, the blaze flared out of control, and a call for help went out to Manhattan, fifteen miles away.

That's when Smoky Joe Martin, New York's legendary fireman, came to the rescue. The short, brawny fifty-nine-year-old deputy chief of the New York Fire Department was one of the first to arrive on the scene. With his white fire helmet cocked a little to the side, he fingered his graying walrus mustache and assessed the situation: Most of Arverne was burning and the huge fire was moving quickly, threatening half a dozen towns further down the Rockaway Peninsula.

Unfortunately, the firefighters were behind the conflagration, which by now had formed a fiery barricade that stretched clear across the peninsula, blocking them from getting in front of the blaze to battle it and protect the other towns in its path. All Smoky Joe had at his disposal at that moment were the town's three fire trucks. Reinforcements were still several minutes from arriving.

Smoky Joe looked for a way around the fire, but there were no other roads; just soft, sandy soil. "Boys, we're going to have to go through the fire," he announced to the young firemen. "We'll get an engine to the other side, then we'll head it off there."

Using the main road meant they would have to breach several solid walls of fire that stood in their way. The toll, Smoky Joe knew, might be his life and the lives of the young men with him. But he saw no alternative.

Over four decades, the veteran smoke-eater had experienced many close calls, including some in which his fellow firemen assumed he had perished in the flames. Each time, though, he rose from the ashes.

Smoky Joe

That's how he got his nickname. One winter night in 1900, then thirty-six-year-old Captain Joe Martin, commander of Engine 31, was fighting a fierce cellar fire in a large building at West and Hubert Streets. The blaze was belching black smoke so thick it obstructed the light from a street lamp just ten feet away.

Despite the efforts of Engine 31, the flames and smoke intensified. One by one the thirty firemen, many gasping for breath in the burning cellar, staggered out on their own or were dragged to safety after losing consciousness.

Soon all the men were out of the building and out of danger, except for Captain Martin, who was last seen manning a hose deep in the cellar. Because of the intensity of the blaze, everyone knew it was futile to attempt a rescue. And everyone knew there was no way he could survive such a fire. "If the flames don't get him, the smoke will," one of his men grimly remarked. "I hope we'll find enough of him to bury."

Hours later, when the flames subsided, Edward Croker, the deeply saddened fire chief, decided he would be the one to retrieve the body of the fallen hero. Croker descended into the basement and followed Martin's hose, hoping it would lead him to the captain's body.

On his hands and knees to avoid the smoke,

Croker straddled the hose in the smoldering ruins until he found Martin face down in the muck between crates of charred furniture. To the chief's utter amazement, Martin's blistered hands had remained wrapped around the hose, which was still spraying water on the lingering flames. But even more astonishing, Martin was still alive!

Grabbing the unconscious, smoke-blackened firefighter by the scruff, Croker hauled Martin up the stairs and outside where he was quickly revived. To a crowd of reporters who had gathered in the assumption they would be writing a story about a hero's death, Croker announced, "Gentlemen, this is 'Smoky Joe' Martin. By the gods, he sure does love his work."

From then on, everyone in the city knew the gutsy, stocky fireman with the hound dog face and walrus mustache as simply Smoky Joe.

Now, as the fire stormed through Arverne, Smoky Joe glanced at the faces of his small band of firefighters and knew he couldn't wait for reinforcements to arrive. He had to act now. He and his men needed to race through walls of flames to have any success of beating back the blaze.

"Fire fighting is war," he told them. "We have to take this chance. It's the only way." He and his crew hopped onto a fire truck. The driver revved the engine and then bolted toward the first wall of

Smoky Joe

flames. Covering their faces, they sped past one flaming barrier, then another and another. They almost made it through to the other side when the truck stalled between the blazes.

"Get the extinguishers! We can't let her burn!" Smoky shouted. The men leaped off, extinguishers in hand, and tried to keep the flames at bay, but soon the extinguishers were spent and useless.

"Push! Let's push it out of the flames!" Smoky Joe bellowed.

The men strained, putting all their might behind the truck as burning ashes fell down on them and flames shot up around them. They mustered a few strong shoves before the truck's metal body became too hot to touch.

Realizing that remaining even a few seconds longer would spell their doom, Smoky Joe gave the order to retreat: "Let's go, boys. We've done all we can here."

They ran for their lives, dodging pockets of fire and falling debris. They sprinted through the thick smoke that was now choking the entire peninsula.

The streets were filled with panicked, screaming residents trying to escape. In their rush to safety, mothers became separated from their children and were darting around in circles, holding their heads, shrieking the names of their lost little ones.

One such girl was sitting on the curb, clutching

a doll and weeping. "There, there, come with me," a firefighter said. He scooped her up into his arms and joined the fleeing crowd.

Smoky Joe put out five alarms. Fireboats were summoned, as were searchlights, because he knew that this battle would last well into the night. Fire companies sped in from all over the area, but it took time. When reinforcements arrived, Smoky Joe boomed, "Glad to see you, boys. I was getting sort of lonesome."

Although the backups were vital, Smoky Joe needed more help, so he rounded up civilian volunteers and put them to work in an effort to save some of the buildings. "Men, you'll have to take a hand," he barked. "Grab buckets and keep those roofs wetted down."

The volunteer bucket brigade sprang into action as residents scrambled to the tops of houses and doused roofs. But flames roared on toward other buildings.

Smoky Joe was horrified to see fire advancing toward the Israel Orphans home where 184 children were huddled inside. He set up a line of firefighters with hoses between the advancing fire and the orphanage. But instead of aiming the water at the fire, they kept their backs to the flames and trained their hoses on the orphanage. They managed to keep the orphanage from bursting in flames until all the children were rescued.

Smoky Joe

The wind was pushing the main fire line southwest toward several small beachfront towns on the peninsula. Smoky Joe knew chances were slim that he could save the villages by continuing to fight the fire from behind.

"We've got to get our trucks through the flames," he told his assistant.

"But we tried that and it failed."

"Yes, but now we have lots of backup. And this time we'll get through because we'll set up a relay."

Smoky Joe's bold plan called for the first fire company to set their hoses and spray water down the street, clearing a path through the flames for the second company, which would then spray water ahead of it so the third company could advance. The third company would clear a path for the first company. This way, they would leapfrog through the town, coming out on the other side where they would then face the inferno head-on and keep it from advancing.

"Let's go!" he yelled, leading the charge up the street. From building to building, hydrant to hydrant, the firefighters ran, setting up their hoses and knocking down the flames so the trucks behind them could advance. But there were setbacks. At one point, the butt of a hydrant was too hot to unscrew. Other times the hoses caught fire. But the firemen didn't give up because the leapfrogging tactic was working. They were breaking through the walls of fire.

After passing the charred shell of the fire truck that had stalled in their earlier attempt, the firefighters were blocked by burning debris. So Smoky ran to the nearest house, ripped a door off its hinges and tossed it to his men. "Here's your shield, boys. Move on!"

They grabbed the door and held it in front of them as they tried to shove the burning debris out of the way. But then their makeshift shield burst into flames. They persevered nevertheless because by now they were close to the front of the fire and near the last of the burning homes.

Smoky Joe was feeling increasingly confident when suddenly, fiery debris from a crumbling building crashed down on him, scorching his face and hands and knocking the wind out of him.

Hurt and burned, the grizzled firefighter flung the red hot embers off his turnout coat, rose to his feet, and tottered toward a fire truck. Over his protests, Smoky Joe was carted off to a field hospital, where he received emergency treatment for his blackened and blistered skin and lacerations.

The doctor wanted to send him to a regular hospital, but Smoky Joe wouldn't hear of it. These injuries were nothing compared to the ones he had suffered back in 1903, when he braved flames and

Smoky Joe

smoke trying to rescue a man assumed trapped (wrongly, it turned out) in a third-floor loft of a burning building on Walker Street. After Smoky Joe kicked down the door and entered the loft, the floor collapsed, sending Smoky plunging all the way into the burning cellar. His men dragged him out and rushed him to the hospital, where doctors expected him to die any minute. Smoky Joe was back on the job in a few weeks.

Although he was in pain from the injuries he sustained in the Arverne fire, he refused further treatment at the field hospital.

"I have to get back to the fire," Smoky Joe asserted.

"You're hurt," the doctor replied. "You have to stay here."

"I'm too busy to be hurt. I have to be with my boys."

With that said, Smoky Joe rejoined the battle, where the turning point had been reached. The firefighters had leapfrogged to the front of the fire and were able to thwart its forward progress. By morning, the flames surrendered.

When Smoky Joe phoned headquarters, he proudly announced, "We got her! Send coffee for the boys."

The devastating fire left ten thousand people homeless, and although it was one of the worst conflagrations in the New York area, not one person perished, thanks in no small part to the skill and bravery of Smoky Joe Martin.

As bad as the Arverne fire was, it wasn't the toughest blaze he fought. That dubious honor went to the Greenpoint Inferno.

It started with a dull thud, something like the underground rumbling of an earthquake that shook the ground for blocks. It was followed by an enormous explosion as a geyser of flame soared hundreds of feet into the air from the top of Tank 36 at the Standard Oil Plant in Greenpoint, Brooklyn, on Saturday afternoon, September 13, 1919.

The tank had been filled with a highly flammable liquid, a white oil used in the manufacture of kerosene. No one knew how the fire started, but everyone knew that it would soon be out of control.

At 2:02 P.M., the first alarm went out and firemen rushed in with hoses. But the streams of water didn't seem to help. In fact, they made the situation worse, spreading the burning oil. Flames danced along the ground from the first tank to the next, which held the same kind of liquid. In seconds, that tank went up with a great roar, its heavy steel wall crumpling in on itself like a paper cup. Smoke and fire shot out the top.

Another tank exploded into flames, then another. Firemen were blown off their feet from the blasts and then showered with burning oil. They covered their eyes, scrambled to their feet, and blindly turned their hoses straight up to the sky, hoping to cool the droplets of hellfire raining from the sky.

"We're just spreading it!" one firefighter yelled as he desperately aimed his hose toward the inferno.

Soon an entire city block was a mass of flames. A second alarm sounded, then a third. Smoke-eaters rushed in, company after company. From all over the city they came and quickly were put to work. Nevertheless, the fire continued to rage out of control.

"Nothing is working. Nothing," lamented Smoky Joe to a fellow deputy chief as they scanned the horrific scene. One by one, his men were forced to retreat. As the fire raced toward them, they fled for their lives. Some screamed in pain, threw themselves on the ground and ripped off their boots because hot oil had penetrated their boots, blistering and burning their feet.

"We're doing all we know how," said Smoky Joe. "It's just not enough. My God, this may be the fire that beats us."

In all his years in the department, Smoky Joe thought he had seen everything. But the inferno at the Standard Oil Field was something new, something more horrible than anything he or any of the other department veterans could ever remember.

Even worse, he wasn't sure what he could do to contain it. "An oil fire has to burn itself out. The best we can hope for is to keep it in check."

Hope of doing that faded as another tank blew up, sending waves of burning oil washing down to the street toward Newtown Creek, a small waterway that bordered the oil yard and separated the boroughs of Queens and Brooklyn.

"My God, if that burning oil flows into the creek and climbs the other bank, we could lose half the city!" Martin declared.

By now a total of twenty-nine tanks had exploded and were spewing flames and belching smoke that formed a black cloud stretching for miles over the city. Smoky Joe called in a fourth alarm and then a fifth, but the fire continued to roar out of control. By 9 P.M., every firefighter, every truck, and every hose in Brooklyn and Queens had been dispatched to the burning oil plant.

Smoky Joe put out two more borough calls, pulling in seventeen engine and four ladder companies from Manhattan. By 10 P.M., he had every available hand working at the blaze, but still it glowed hot and red against the night sky. Close to the fire it was like daytime. In Hades.

All other options were gone when Smoky Joe sent out the 6-6-6-6 alarm, a call of desperation that had never been heard before in the city: "Fire out of

Smoky Joe

control. Send everyone and everything." Soon every available firefighter, whether on duty or off, rushed to the fire. Nearly five thousand men were engaged fully in a pitched battle with the enormous blaze.

But their efforts seemed in vain.

The advancing fire—its heat so intense it was melting bricks in the street—relentlessly pushed the firefighters back toward Newtown Creek. Soon the flames were threatening to jump across to the other side and spread their fiery destruction into the residential areas a few hundred yards from the waterway. In the fire's path were lines of wood-frame working-class houses—four- and five-story walk-ups crammed with families and children.

Meanwhile, the fire struck the oil plant's steam pipes. Flames soon seared off the asbestos coverings and melted the pipes, causing boiling hot water and steam to cascade upon the front line firefighters.

Men overcome by fumes and smoke or burned or scalded by fire and steam were rushed to makeshift field hospitals. "They're falling all over the place!" Smoky Joe shouted, helplessly watching his men go down. As if this wasn't enough, he needed to deal with another difficult problem: human curiosity.

Thousands of gawkers from nearby neighborhoods were crowding the street along Kingston Avenue. "Damn! They must think this is the Fourth of July," he snarled to an assistant. "We must clear them out of there. They're going to get themselves killed—and take us with them if we have to rescue them."

But it was too late. No sooner had Smoky Joe finished the thought than the wind shifted, sending flames racing toward the mob. Flying embers began setting women's hair and men's hats ablaze. The once curious crowd was now a shrieking, panic-stricken horde running wildly in all directions.

Smoky Joe gasped when he saw a little boy being trampled after he tripped and fell while trying to keep up with terror-crazed adults running for their lives. An older man dove into the rushing throng hoping to save the boy but ended up being trampled himself. Fire Lieutenant John Burns tried to rescue them both, only to suffer the same fate.

Turning to two nearby firefighters, Smoky Joe ordered, "Follow me, boys! Let's get in there and help them before they're all crushed!"

While Smoky Joe, acting like an offensive line-man guarding his quarterback, fended off the uncontrollable mob, one fireman swept up the child and the other dragged the older man, who was seriously injured, out from under the stampede.

"That's the way, boys!" Smoky Joe shouted as he kept blocking for Burns until the lieutenant managed to haul himself out of the way despite a shattered leg.

Smoky Joe

Smoky Joe was trying to catch his breath and think up new tactics to stop the fire from spreading when he saw a row of tenement houses burst into flames.

"We got everybody out of there, didn't we?" he asked one of his men.

"Yes, sir."

"Then let's pull back. We can't save those buildings."

"Look, look! There's a woman and a baby!" yelled someone in the crowd that had formed near the fire-fighters for protection. "She's up in the window, the third floor!"

"Hold it, boys," Smoky Joe ordered. "We can't retreat. We have to save them."

The flames were moving closer and he knew that he and his brave crew would be goners if their hoses or their luck gave out. The men stood firm and kept their hoses aimed at the building where the woman and her infant were trapped.

The woman, sure she would die, was weeping and begging anyone who could hear her to save her baby. "She's only a day old. Don't let her die like this! Save her! Don't worry about me."

"We'll get them out!" a lieutenant yelled as he led half a dozen young men under the stream of water that was barely keeping the hungry flames at bay.

"Go get 'em, boys! Don't abandon them to the

flames!" Smoky Joe bellowed through the megaphone he used to give commands.

Within seconds a firefighter appeared at the window behind the still screaming mother and grabbed her around the waist. Another fireman snatched the baby from her arms. In an instant the window was empty. Moments later, the new mother and her infant were safely behind the battle lines.

Miraculously, the wind changed directions again, forcing the wall of fire to draw back over ground that had already been burned. With the help of the wind, the firemen were finally able to beat the fire into submission on the banks of Newtown Creek, saving most of the tenement houses.

But the blaze continued to flare at the oil yard. Tanks kept exploding, spewing burning droplets of oil that ignited the ground when they landed. Firemen manning the hoses were forced to leap around as the very spots they were standing on burst into foul-smelling flames.

"Twenty acres of hell," Smoky Joe muttered before dealing with the next crisis.

A stream of red-hot oil flowed toward a 50,000-gallon tank that rested on a 100-foot steel tower. Smoky Joe ordered the hoses turned toward the tower in a desperate effort to cool it while hopefully thwarting the advance of the burning oil stream.

The water held the flames back for a few minutes,

but the fire was too strong and reached the tower. In seven minutes, the steel legs of the tower began to melt and buckle.

"Get out of there! She's going down!" Smoky Joe hollered. Firemen dropped their hoses and scattered as the tower collapsed, sending the enormous tank plunging down onto a warehouse next door.

As fate would have it, the warehouse was a storage site for hundreds of steel drums holding thousands of gallons of gin and alcohol. Seconds later, those steel drums began exploding, flying into the air like huge fireballs, then bursting apart hundreds of feet up and showering hot fragments on the firemen below, including Smoky Joe.

His face singed and swelling, he staggered with his men toward a Red Cross tent, where nurses soothed the firemen's eyes with cotton pads. After a brief five-minute break, Smoky Joe hurried back out to direct his men in another assault on the burning oil depot.

It took nearly two days, but the fire department, which reported sixty-five injured firemen, finally knocked down the blaze. Incredibly, thanks to Smoky Joe's leadership, no firefighter or civilian was killed.

Smoky Joe stayed in the department for forty-six years until a heart attack forced him into retirement in 1930, when he was sixty-seven. But his passion for fighting fires was so strong that for years after, he often followed the fire trucks on their runs, sometimes incognito. He died in 1941 at the age of seventy-eight.

The presence of Smoky Joe Martin is still felt today. In his honor, the United States Forest Service named (with a slight change in spelling) their firefighting mascot "Smokey the Bear."